2/14

PSALM 44

OTHER WORKS BY DANILO KIŠ IN ENGLISH TRANSLATION

The Attic
Garden, Ashes
Early Sorrows
Hourglass
A Tomb for Boris Davidovich
The Encyclopedia of the Dead
Homo Poeticus: Essays and Interviews
The Lute and the Scars

PSALM 44

DANILO KIŠ

Preface by Aleksandar Hemon

Translated and with an Afterword
by John K. Cox

DALKEY ARCHIVE PRESS
CHAMPAIGN • DUBLIN • LONDON

Originally published in Serbian as *Psalam 44* by Globus, Zagreb, 1962
Psalam 44 by Danilo Kiš © Librairie Arthème Fayard and Danilo Kiš Estate.
Preface copyright © 2012 by Aleksandar Hemon
Translation and afterword copyright © 2012 by John K. Cox
First edition, 2012

Library of Congress Cataloging-in-Publication Data

Kiš, Danilo, 1935-1989.
[Psalam 44. English]
Psalm 44 / Danilo Kiš ; preface by Aleksandar Hemon ; translated and with an afterword by John K. Cox.
    p. cm.
Includes bibliographical references.
ISBN 978-1-56478-762-0 (cloth : alk. paper)
  1. Auschwitz (Concentration camp)--Fiction. I. Hemon, Aleksandar, 1964- II. Cox, John K., 1964- III. Title.
PG1419.21.I8P7713 2012
891.8'2354--dc23
                          2012013731

This translation has been published with the financial support of the Serbian Ministry of Culture

Supported using public funding by the National Lottery through Arts Council England

Partially funded by grants from the National Endowment for the Arts, a federal agency, and the Illinois Arts Council, a state agency

www.dalkeyarchive.com

Cover: design and composition by Mikhail Iliatov

Printed on permanent/durable acid-free paper and bound in the United States of America

CONTENTS

PREFACE

Let me start with a complaint: What is absent from much of contemporary fiction, which in the USA is conceived of as middle-to-highbrow entertainment, is the ethical import of literature. As it is, the word fiction largely stands for (deliberately) made-up narratives aiming to entertain the culturally enlightened reader. Literature, on the other hand, is nothing if not continuous ethical and aesthetical engagement with human experience and history; one reads/writes literature in order to confront the hard questions of human existence; entertainment might not be applicable. While the word fiction equally applies to *The Da Vinci Code* and *Remembrance of Things Past*, only one of those is literature; the other one is trash. ("Do not argue that all values are relative: there is a hierarchy of values," Kiš wrote in his "Advice to a Young Writer.") American populism of the knee-jerk variety requires cringing at the thought of literature (and, for that matter, at any thought that is not confirming what is already agreed to be true), because it is—what is the word flung about by the humble sons of the one percent?—elitist. (Kiš's advice: "Do not write for an elite that does not exist: you are the elite.") But literature is inherently democratic, as it is the way for everyone and anyone who can read to enter the difficult and vast field of *everything* that comes under humanity. "Do not write for 'the average reader,'" Kiš wrote to the Young Writer, "all readers are average."

In the home of the brave, literature has been damaged, perhaps irreparably, by the systematic avoidance of difficulty, by the cultural laziness that spreads like brain-infecting flu out of the sunny realm of eternal, unconditional entertainment. Bullied by the cryptofascist, consumerist resistance to public thought—or thinking in public—American literature tends to avoid uncomfortable weight: the weight of tradition; the weight of civic and historical responsibility; the weight of language, which needs to be ceaselessly reinvented and reevaluated. The ethical fiascoes of the Bush era in perpetuity unfettered, the catastrophic wars and the insidious fantasies that prepared them and maintain them, the widespread collapse of the notion of a socially-responsible government and the related (reality-based) democracy, the rabid xenophobia indistinguishable from the socially-acceptable practices of American Patriotism, the mind-crushing lies reproducing the belief that capitalism is the best thing ever—all have been pretty much ignored in our contemporary fiction. Not many American authors know how to confront the history we're living in; few attempt to, even fewer dare to claim an ethically/aesthetically-defined system of thought that would demand from the reader to engage with the difficulties of the early twenty-first century.

The reason for writing from a confrontational position would be less in the necessity for social engagement ("At the mention of 'engaged literature' be silent as a fish: leave it to the professors," Kiš advised) than in the fact that recent history ought to be seen as a fertile creative ground, as an ethical and aesthetical opportunity, a chance to loosen the unstimulating grip of epiphanic psychological realism. Much of American literature has been paralyzed, producing nary a novel that would fundamentally—ethically, aesthetically—question and take apart the *Matrix*-like reality of what is commonly referred to as America. We need a literature that would do the difficult work of finding meaning beyond what is offered as self-evident ("Do not believe in statistics, figures, or public statements: reality is what the naked eye cannot see.") and counter the steady production of systemic oblivion. It might turn out to be difficult; we might have to learn how to do it from writers like Danilo Kiš. As it is now, there seems to be a consensus that any whiff of difficulty coming from the contemporary novel would result in the already depleted literary readership retreating deeper into the mindless territories of Iron Men and the many shades of gray.

The greatness of Kiš's work lies in his unflinching willingness to confront and (re)imagine the horrors of history as experienced by human beings. The aim of his work is not to bear witness ("Have no mission," Kiš advises. "Beware of people with missions.") but to reconfirm the value of individual experience; he is not merely reporting on the state of individual humanity, rather, he recreates it in language, thereby reestablishing its sovereignty, without which the very project of literature is inconceivable.

His relation with—or, rather, his position within—history was defined by his traumatic personal experience: as a child he witnessed the Novi Sad massacre in the winter of 1942 (to which frequently returns in his work, *Psalm 44* included), when Hungarian fascists slaughtered a large number of Jews and Serbs; his family was persecuted and spent the war displaced in Hungary; his father disappeared in Auschwitz. But his engagement is just as intensely intellectual: the question of how one could (and why one would) write novels after Auschwitz and Kolyma (the Stalinist camp) was a burning one for him throughout his working life. ("Should anyone tell you Kolyma was different from Auschwitz," he told the Young Writer, "tell him to go to hell.") He, of course, kept on writing, but the perpetual doubt about the purpose of writing required a continuous reevaluation of the ethical and aesthetical foundations of literature.

Each of his books has a distinctly different structure, but his quest was not for an abstractly perfect literary form. What he kept looking for was *any form at all* that could match and contain the intensity, fragmentariness, intellectual weight, and troubling connotations of modern history, as well as the sheer pain and sorrow it has generated. If Kiš was a postmodernist, it was out of painful necessity. His inclination to construct difficult narrative structures was not a consequence of his highfalutin whimsy but rather of a deeply held conviction that he needed to (re)discover and (re)deploy narrative techniques ("Study the thought of others, then reject it," he instructed the Young Writer) that could match the horrific intricacies of the twentieth century and his personal experience in it. Thus his masterpieces *Garden, Ashes* and *Hourglass* (both, with *Early Sorrows*, part of a novelistic family cycle or, per

Kiš, "the family circus") have a perishing father at the absent center, but are constructed markedly differently. Both novels could be described as "experimental" in the lazy cant of critics baffled by any form outside the cramped confines of psychological realism, but *Garden, Ashes* harkens back to Bruno Schulz and his prophetically mad father, while *Hourglass* is structured as an interrogation, featuring, in one of the most heartbreaking structural devices in the twentieth-century literature, a letter Kiš's father sent to the family before he was deported to Auschwitz.

Kiš's ethical/aesthetical system (there is no dissociation between ethics and aesthetics in his mind) is founded on the axiomatic value of individual sovereignty. That sovereignty is universal—every human being is entitled to it—and is continuously and brutally violated by history. Thus the uniqueness of his father's experience, including his particular path to ovens of Auschwitz, is exactly related to the uniqueness of the forms Kiš reinvents to restore his father's invaluable life, destroyed by those who did not believe in the sanctity of individual sovereignty.

Kiš wrote *Psalm 44* at the age of twenty-five, in less than a month, in order to submit it to the contest of the Association of Jewish Communities in Yugoslavia. He had come across a newspaper story about a young couple revisiting a camp where their child was born and decided to write about it; he could do it, because he "could accept a somewhat unusual plot as factual." He was writing at the same time his novel *The Attic*, which was entirely different in form and spirit. The two short books would be published in the same volume in Belgrade in 1962.

The mastery of Kiš's structural—and therefore aesthetical—choices at such a young age is most impressive. The young man's creative confidence is sharply evident in his undertaking a narrative project that

a) takes place in a death camp;

b) focuses on women, one of whom has given birth in the camp;

c) exhibits near-arrogant familiarity with the history of European thought, its ethical decline and collapse included;

d) is mostly set in the few hours before an escape attempt;

e) refuses to avoid the moral and structural challenges inherent in the situation.

Psalm 44 thus augured the arrival of a major talent, even if few could see that Kiš would be among the twentieth century's essential writers. One shudders to think what masterpieces—in addition to, at least, *A Tomb for Boris Davidovich*; *Garden, Ashes*; *Hourglass*; and *The Encyclopedia of the Dead*—Kiš would have produced had he not been stricken by cancer at the age of fifty-four. The Nobel Prize committee had already been circling around him and, had he not died, his great works would have been available to a much larger number of readers, influencing young writers all across the globe.

One of the ways to diagnose the greatness of a literary work is to identify the moments or details that stop you in your tracks and demand to be thought through, forcing you to adjust your readerly expectations. Those are the moments that might make the work difficult, necessarily countering the page-turning consumerist instincts. Great works effectively train you how to read them, generating a thought process that might well extend beyond reading the book. *Psalm 44*, slight though it may be, is rife with such mind-stopping instances. Take Maks, the übersurvivor, the genocide superhero, "a devilishly clever fellow," the belief in whom seems to have been induced by the utter hopelessness of the camp. Or the directness of naming the Mengele-like camp "scientist" Dr. Nietzsche, bringing up in one brazen move a whole set of ethical questions about "science" and its role in the extermination of European Jewry, as well as about the complicity of philosophy in the Nazis' apocalyptic reconstitution of history. Or the wet concreteness of diapers for Jan, a child born in the camp, whose mother, Marija, is drying them against her body. Or Marija's obsessive thinking about the sheet she takes from Polya, the dying woman, as she is trying to decide at what point Polya will no longer need it. Or Marija's memories of the Novi Sad massacre, which Kiš conveys in a few terrifying details, so that the terror is as fully experienced as it can be in a work of literature.

All those moments are contained by a structure that deliberately slows down time. The main temporal framework of the novel is delimited by the few hours before Marija and her fellow inmate attempt a courageous escape from the camp, as the cannons of the Allied forces are thundering in the distance; within those few hours much is recollected, no tranquility whatsoever available. Kiš writes in long, convoluted crypto-Proustian sentences, which allow him to follow closely Marija's thoughts, thus making each terrible and hopeful moment count.

Kiš's ethical ambition is even more impressive than his aesthetical/technical repertoire or the brilliance of his details. As someone who has taught creative writing classes and has often dealt with works teeming with ailing grandparents, suburban boredom, and college-love breakups, I long for a student who would write with Kišian intellectual and moral confidence, or, at least, urgency. I long for a young American writer who would, like Kiš, in his or her first book, present the case that literature is capable of processing the most difficult human experiences, be they personal or historical—it is one of the few tools (and, for some of us, the only one) we have to get a handle on life and history. Writing fiction can be taught and practiced, but what cannot be taught and practiced is ethical courage. "If you cannot say the truth," Kiš advised the Young Writer, "say nothing."

At a very young age, Kiš understood the nature of willful forgetfulness and the role it plays in the history as narrated by the powers that be. He saw literature as capable of forestalling oblivion, of telling the history experienced by individual human beings. Everyone who has ever suffered had a name, a set of parents, a life comprised of a multitude of irreplaceable details; the death of each one of us is an irreparable loss to all of humanity. That seems like an easy kind of knowledge to acquire, but many—writers, artists, politicians, killers, historians—have failed to fully comprehend the infinite weight of a single human life and the enormous price we pay in oblivion for each one extinguished. "Because that's what death is, *To forget everything*," Marija, Kiš's hero, realizes in *Psalm 44*. The only way to remember what must be remembered is to tell the stories of lives that have been erased by the megalomaniacal callousness of history. Such stories might be difficult to construct and read, but they are ethically and aesthetically necessary. Without them we will be forgotten. Without them we are nothing on our way to nothing.

Aleksandar Hemon, 2012

PSALM 44

"And the angel of the LORD said unto her, Behold, thou art with child, and shalt bear a son, and shalt call his name Ishmael; because the LORD hath heard thy affliction."

—THE FIRST BOOK OF MOSES

"Thou makest us a byword among the heathen . . ."

—PSALM 44

1

For several days already, people had been whispering the news that she was going to attempt an escape before the camp was evacuated. Especially once (and this had happened five or six nights earlier) the thundering of artillery had first become audible in the distance. But then the whispering had died down somewhat—at least it seemed that way to her—since those three other women had been killed on the wire. One of them was Eržika Kon, who'd shared the same barracks.

That's why all she could do now was listen intently to the cannon and wait for something to happen. She felt every bit as capable of doing something (if only she knew what it was—like, for example those lightbulbs that they knocked down with a stick last night as if they were pears dangling from the arbor in their garden, though it was only thanks to Žana that she was able to do that, thanks to being led by her, because it never would have occurred to her personally to smash lightbulbs and to think of it as anything other than an unnecessary risk, as suicide) as Polja probably felt, Polja who was now lying delirious next to her in the straw. Marija could only wait for Žana to tell her *now* (in the same way she had until now been saying "not yet," or less than that, really: only "we'll see" or "we'll do something all right"), and then she'd take her child in her arms like a piece of luggage filled with valuables that one had to spirit unseen out the rear entrance right under the noses of the agents who knew that those purloined valuables were about to be removed and probably through that very door. And whenever Žana finally told her it was time, she would take that camouflaged and deliberately inconspicuous suitcase and walk with it through the cordon of agents and police officers, desperately resolved to pass unobserved and proceeding precisely as she'd been told and ordered to act, conscious of her obligation to her instructions, for in this moment (if something unforeseen were to occur), if someone came up to her from behind (let's say) and tapped on her shoulder to ask her to show her bag, her only defense, the only one she could think up in time, would be to shield the precious bundle, the child, with her own body, perhaps harboring the secret and irrational hope into the bargain that the ground underneath her would open up in that moment and that she would find herself down below in some shadowy courtyard where, with a nod of his head, a *deus ex machina* would introduce himself to her: that would be Maks. For Maks, invisible and omnipresent, was going to appear and intervene decisively, and the fact that he had already committed himself to the escape—that much had been clear to her from the first instant. Actually from the time (and that was three evenings ago) that Žana had brought hope into the barracks, the hope concealed in her eyes, and she'd said in a whisper that "all is not lost." And indeed all was not lost. Though Polja was lying in her delirium for a third day on account of malaria and people kept expecting them to come take her away at any moment; it was incomprehensible that they hadn't taken her away that very first evening when she came back sick and feeble. Perhaps they were showing her (Polja) a little extra consideration on account of her playing cello in the prisoners' orchestra, right at the entrance to the gas chamber (or so people said) for such a long time; or else—and this was more likely—because of the rapid advance of the Allies and the booming of those heavy guns, ever nearer, forcing the commanders of the camp to postpone any further executions.

That evening Žana returned to the barracks a little late. It was a wet November night, ice cold, and the grim wind carried the worn and ill-tuned sounds of the prisoners' orchestra playing Beethoven's *Eroica* as well as the camp tune "The Girl I Adore." Polja was still babbling unintelligibly. In Russian. Dying. No one dared light a lamp and Žana made her way, groping, over to her bunk (she oriented herself by Polja's death rattle). Marija feared that Polja, however, was beyond hearing. Then she freed her child from the straw and rags in which it was sleeping: a little wax doll. Marija didn't dare get too close to Polja. She feared for her child. And for herself. His mother.

The sound of Žana's steps reached her ears: this liberated her from thoughts of Polja. And then all at once it dawned on her with great conviction that something must have happened. Whatever it was that had held Žana up this long. A message from Jakob. Or from Maks. ("That Maks" was undoubtedly up to something. Present but invisible.) But Žana said nothing. Marija only heard her light, conspiratorial footsteps. (Suddenly this seemed extremely odd to her: Žana had still not taken off her boots.) Then the rustling of straw, the dull thud of her heavy boots shed, the rusty sound of the tin can of water, and once more the rustling of straw, this time over by Polja, and then: the slight clinking of Polja's teeth against the can. Marija wanted, in vain, to give some sort of signal, to say something about Polja, not only to express her doubt that she could accompany them on their journey but also to say at last what both she and Žana had known since the first day Polja came back sick, the thing that hovered between them unstated but certain: *Polja is going to die.* But Žana emancipated Marija from that responsibility and she heard her give a whisper that was eerily like listening to another person give voice to your own newborn thought:

"*Elle va mourir à l'aube!*" Žana said.

Marija merely sighed in response. She felt her throat constricting. As if she were only now becoming aware—just now when Žana said it—of what she herself had already accepted since the day Polja had come back ill: she was going to die. Now Polja's discordant rambling seemed more audible than the distant song of the big guns. That's the reason Marija had wanted to start up a conversation with Žana and have her talk about the cannons, about Jakob, about the escape, ultimately about anything, just so that it would set her free from this nightmare and so that she wouldn't hear Polja's death rattle, so that she wouldn't think about how even after she was dead nothing was going to happen, not now not afterward not in two or in two hundred twenty-two days—just as nothing had happened up to this point; no running away, no Jakob, no Maks, not even any cannons, nothing was going to happen except that same thing which was happening here and now to Polja: she was fading slowly, spluttering, as a candle gutters and goes out.

The rhythmic beaming of the floodlights that entered through a crack in the wall tore again and again, clawlike, at the darkness of the barracks, and Marija caught sight of Žana as she stood between a beam of light and the wall; she stepped into it as if to join the illumination and then disappeared again into the darkness. From there, out of that momentarily illuminated darkness, she could hear her voice, her whisper, which like a focused beam of light cut the silence:

"Jan . . . How is Jan?"

"He went to sleep," Marija answered. "He's sleeping." But that wasn't what she'd thought she was going to hear from Žana, she'd expected something different, something completely different than the question *Jan . . . How is Jan?* and she was even certain that Žana had something else to say and it even seemed to her that when Žana greeted her in a whisper, and even before that point, when Žana had still only been thinking of speaking (and it had seemed to the listener that she knew exactly the instant when Žana would start to talk and shatter the silence), that she was going to say something else, for she had to say something completely different, something that (nevertheless) would not be unrelated to this issue; it even struck her now, suddenly (more from the pounding of her pulse than from an actual understanding), that the question *Jan . . . How is Jan?* didn't differ in essence from the question that Žana really needed to ask. Thus—wondering whether it's possible to give a whisper even a tiny measure of nuanced differentiation, but wanting nonetheless to make clear that she's grasped the fact that Žana has something else to say, and that this answer of Marija's is also nothing more than a preliminary—she gave Žana a status report:

"I washed his diapers. Now I'm drying them. I stretched them out down there, and he's lying on top of me, here," as if Žana could see the slight signal from her hand with which she wanted to say: up here, on my chest. "That's why I wasn't in a position to do anything about Polja," but she immediately regretted saying that, not because it wasn't the truth, but because it seemed to her that doing so had sliced the thread and diverted Žana's thoughts from what was important; or at least that doing so had postponed by a moment or so Žana's saying what she still needed to say.

"Poor Polja," Žana said; but it could just as well have been (at least so it seemed to her) "Poor Marija" or "Poor Jan"; and Marija became completely engrossed in the following thought: was it all the same whether Žana said *Poor Jan* or *Poor Marija*? For if that too were a matter of indifference, it would mean that nothing had happened and that nothing was happening. *Polja can't go with us*: she pretended that she was thinking this for the first time and that she was only now grasping the gravity of the whole situation, but all she said was:

"She didn't regain consciousness the whole day."

Then Žana said: "It's better for her . . . Understand?" Her opinion once more in four words of black crystal; and then immediately: "I'd like it to happen as soon as possible. Understand? As soon as possible."

Finally something had been said that retied the sliced thread into a knot and Marija sensed that this once again meant something, something different and something more than the bitter and straightforward truth *Polja is going to die* or *Polja will not be able to come with us,* for it also meant *We are going to go* or at least we will *attempt* it. And she rebelled against the slow birth of a truth already obvious and it seemed to her even a little bit hypocritical that not one of them would admit to herself that they had reconciled themselves to this truth—the fact that they would attempt an escape without Polja—and that this had already been decided and determined not by their wills or by common agreement but simply, terrifyingly and simply, *decided* and nothing else now remained for them to do beyond acquiescing (or not acquiescing, it was all the same) with this fact.

"She won't be able to come with us," Marija said, attempting—even if she wasn't conscious of it—to condense every part of the nightmare into this single sentence that she could get out in one breath the same way that one tries to choke down a bitter pill or poison with one swallow. So she said it hoping to help Žana say once and for all what she needed to say or to do what she had planned or was considering doing, but Žana watched doggedly through the crack in the plank, until she said, as if giving out a slightly altered echo of her own words:

"That's why I want it to happen as soon as possible. You understand: it'll be easier," but then she (Marija) wanted to completely unburden her conscience of these accusations that weighed heavier and heavier upon her and now upon Žana too and she thought, *Perhaps Žana is thinking something out right now and perhaps nothing has happened* but really things only gave her that impression because she wanted them to be that way, just as she likewise wanted something to happen because she knew that it wasn't possible to wait any longer—the cannons were slowly de-

molishing the concrete parapet of passive anticipation and resignation to fate. But then—as soon as she heard Žana's voice, to
try to calm herself down, for she knew that she wouldn't be able
to get to sleep tonight, at least not until Žana said what she was
thinking—she said:

"I'm going to try to sleep," and then—as if doing so would has-
ten the answer and ultimately the decision about which Žana was
thinking and in the absence of which it didn't seem to her (Marija)
that she could think of anything else or do anything else, not until
whatever it was came out, whatever it was concerning herself and
those three other women, for little Eržika Kon had been among
them at first, Eržika Kon who had earlier, one night, hurled herself
at the wire and fallen, riddled with bullets, forgetting everything,
because that's what death is, *To forget everything*, she thought—
she asked: "What time could it be?" as if through this question the
hand of death or at least its sister would be summoned to close her
tired eyes, but with this question resistance was born in her consciousness, as a consequence of some dim recollection of the ultimate interconnectedness of forgetting-death-sleep-and-time and
her consciousness, which set this whole causal chain in motion
and must rank highest in its hierarchy, hand-in-hand with time.

"I don't know," Žana said, but then, as if resistance had been
awakened in her too, she went on to say, as though picking up a
forgotten weapon: "I think it's past eleven. I don't think it's any
later than that." Then like a buoy it popped up to the surface, that
which until this moment had filled the gloom and which now all
at once crystallized and condensed into the space of two or three
words in a whisper: "Tonight we'll try."

And even before Marija succeeded in turning her thoughts to

anything specific, to being fearful or overjoyed, to crying out or to screaming or all of it together in the inferno that was the tumult of her mind and the chaos of her organism, in the savage circulation of blood that cascaded throughout her body like some hot, interior wave leaving behind on the shore the broken and disordered remnants of thought (only the briefest glance at the innumerable associations that were saturating and trampling each other) as well as the secretions of her glands and ovaries—even before she managed to realize that she was trembling on the edge of unconsciousness in this intense assault, Žana added what it was no longer necessary to say: "I didn't want to tell you right away. I was thinking you should get some sleep. You need to be fresh."

In that way she kept Marija from thinking about Polja and from feeling sorry for her, or repentant: Žana had with her words simply wiped Polja away by not mentioning her; she didn't even refer to her as "Poor Polja," which again would have signified something; instead she simply said *we will try*, and in this *we* nothing and no one else could be present save the three of them, that is, Žana, Jan, and Marija: to wit, only the living, and Polja was already beneath a shroud. But Marija could still sense Polja, not because of her quiet gurgling, which was no longer communication in any earthly language but simply a slight whisper in the tongue of death itself; rather Marija could sense her through the fact that she was obliged constantly to push Polja's corpse to the side, out of the current of her own thoughts, down under the ice (they had already buried Polja), just as they had shoved under the Danube's ice the corpses of those women, back then, at the beginning—so that she could make room for the living or at least for those she hoped were living: for Jakob, in fact; who else? And she now all at once caught a glimpse of Jakob—it was the first time she'd pictured him since their last meeting—no longer in the perspective that revealed itself, forlorn and grim, behind her when she looked back at him, but rather in some future, almost imaginable: Jakob stands there, just like that, tall and pale, his face covered in a reddish beard, worn down and worn out from his return but with his eyes radiating happiness and his arms open wide and stretching down the road toward where she's standing, Jan in her arms, offering Jakob the child like bread and salt, like the sacred miracle at Bethlehem. But that momentarily glimpsed perspective on the future began to collapse immediately like a canvas backdrop thrown up in the desert—and only Jakob himself remained in that real wilderness from which the wind had carried off the set, abandoned save for gray drifts of dust.

She thought back to that last meeting with Jakob, not so long ago, actually five weeks ago, Jan was barely two weeks old at that point, no more. She recalled clearly that Jan had been two weeks old: she had given birth on the same day that she saw Jakob for the first time after their separation. But that was further back. She saw Jakob (who else could it have been) a second time back there at the train station; and this is how it was: from Maks she had received a message (she had found the message in the barracks, beneath the headrest in the straw) stating that Jakob would be walking past with a transport, that evening, around seven. She subsequently spent the whole day pondering how she could get away from the worksite and make it to the station to see Jakob and tell him that he was becoming a father and then when she cried out JAKOB, I AM PREGNANT she couldn't have been imagining it and she knew that he had to have heard her cry and recognized her voice, for who else would shout that out to him and do so from the formation that was already approaching the entrance to the camp; hence she had to see Jakob, if not on account of that other thing at least so that she could convince herself that he was alive and so that she could ask him what he thought of all this while he hammered on that coffin at the camp gates and couldn't he have at least stopped swinging the hammer in his hand so that she would at least see that he had heard that she had yelled to him that she was pregnant. And then something unexpected appeared, right when she was thinking in her despair that the only thing she could do was to throw down her shovel all of a sudden and run for it, which would have been pure suicide, and she was already envisioning how she'd fall, shredded by the machine guns, breathing her last, seized with spasms, attempting to pronounce the words "Jakob, Jakob" through the blood rushing out of her mouth, as if he would be able to hear and understand that she was trying that she was doing everything she could that she wanted nothing other than to see him.

That was when a *kapo* ordered Eržika Kon and her to head for the station and deliver something there. She didn't know if this order was genuine or if it was only one of Maks's tricks to make it possible for her to run into Jakob, but she set off toward the station with Eržika Kon, accompanied by a soldier who walked in lockstep with them. She still did not know (and even to this day has not found out) if this had simply been some subterfuge on the part of Maks to enable a meeting with Jakob or if it was mere happenstance that she was summoned from the group and told to go to the depot.

On the way she was wondering if this transport, supposedly containing Jakob, was going to make a stop in the station or just pass through, but she was utterly incapable of doing anything, although she knew that everything beyond this point depended on her and that she had no idea what time it was nor could she inquire of anyone what time it was, although it did appear to her that the time was at hand (they were walking along the new road that the camp inmates had built and she several times considered asking the soldier what time it was but then she took fright at the thought of putting everything at risk and forfeiting the opportunity that had come her way for her to see Jakob) and from that she concluded that Maks had had a hand in all this, but she didn't know if they needed to hurry up or slow their stride even though the soldier was dictating their pace.

And so all at once she found herself at the station, looking at the long row of sealed cars out of which peered phantomlike faces at the small grated windows and she recognized the Babel of cries for help that she herself had heard at the time she was transported in cattle cars of that same type, that outcry which becomes a dry and morbid whisper: in all the languages of Europe the word *water* being pronounced as if it were the very stuff of life, even more so than that ancient Hellenic *ur*-element and essential substance belonging to every living thing, along with air and earth, of course—the way that word now transformed itself on Polja's lips, the chaos of the cattle car shrinking to the monotone whisper of a moribund. And then the train moved just as she caught sight of it, right in front of her nose like some enormous antediluvian dinosaur ejected from its watery home onto firm dry land several millennia after its epoch, and she sensed all at once the thirst in Jakob's guts and in her own and she began to run down the line of cars, now starting to rock, and they collided with a bang and she was like a condemned soul having her guts gnawed out by the plague and she was utterly transformed into screaming into the cry into "Jakob! Jakob!" as if that reptile were beginning to rouse itself and make a getaway, gasping for breath, completely metamorphosed into that stegocephalian dinosaurian Babylonian and European "Water! Water!" and suddenly she saw a rag appear from a high, narrow window of the car ten meters in front of her, like a *reliquiae reliquiarum* of Jakob, and after that the hand holding that rag and waving it like death's own flag—that clenched hand without a face, motioning with the rag—that was Jakob now, the Jakob who had remained when with a bang the stage and set had been destroyed and she looked backward: gray drifts of dust.

But Žana was still going on:

"Maks's orders," she said, not waiting for the flood of blood inside Marija to ebb, the blood that was pounding her and rocking her off her foundations: "Tonight at 2:30," she said. "Get prepared and try to get some sleep. You need to be rested. I'll wait for Maks's signal: two long and two short knocks."

"Okay. I'll try," Marija responded. "I'll try to sleep at least a bit."

2

Žana lay on her stomach in the straw, propped up on her elbows, head thrust between her palms; her legs trembled slightly. Chewing on a short piece of straw, she looked out through the crack in the direction of the fence. Periodically a fine edge of light slid across her face and tore open the intense darkness of the barracks; then Marija, without moving her head or disturbing the baby asleep on top of her, could see Žana's profile with that straw in her mouth.

"She'll be dead by dawn," Marija said, but her voice made itself heard against her will; and then as if meant for herself: "I should return this sheet to Polja." She heard Žana's suppressed sigh and thought *That is an answer*, but right away she caught another whisper:

"So much the better for her. You understand: *tomorrow it will be harder to die*. Even in an hour or two it's going to be harder"; and then, "It's already hard enough to die."

"Because of hoping?" Marija asked.

"I don't know," Žana replied. "Maybe because of hoping." Then she got up and Marija realized, although she didn't see it, that Žana had risen to give Polja the can with water; "Now it's a human being that's dying," Žana said. "You understand: a human being and not an animal."

Then Marija repeated what she had said a short while before, but she wasn't thinking of that, she was already thinking *I should return the sheet to Polja* and she was wondering if Polja could hear the artillery and she was thinking it would be better if Polja couldn't hear it, but all she said was:

"Yes, it's on account of hope"; and Žana repeated:

"Up to now it was an animal dying. It's easier, I believe, to die like that."

The other woman didn't respond. All she felt was the way her body was going numb from lying there, immobile, in the damp: the wet diapers she had wrapped around her naked body were releasing an icy moisture that her skin was absorbing from her stomach to the middle of her thighs; it gave the impression that her skin had become pasty and rotten like that of a corpse, although she didn't really feel like she had skin at all anymore, rather just some gelatinous mass, which together with the wet rags was glued to her bones. But the child wasn't cold; she thought: I folded Polja's sheet over twice and laid it across the wet diapers so that the moisture wouldn't reach the baby. *I didn't dare put the wet diapers on my stomach,* she thought. *I could only wrap them around my thighs, and I didn't dare take off my underwear; it wouldn't be good if I got my period now. It's always so unpredictable; a few sniffles are enough to bring it on*; then she thought that it would be best if she got up and moved the diapers a bit lower. It was probably just past ten now, and Maks was going to give the signal after two, and then she would have to move and she was frightened by the prospect of her legs completely freezing up and turning into some icy, inert mass.

Thus it was necessary to undertake something, above all to push those damp diapers lower and to return the sheet to Polja. But then, on the very cusp of the movement with which she wanted to raise the infant off of herself and to position him so she could stretch her limbs and give Polja back the sheet, she stopped, restrained the movement that was almost finished being born, feeling the way its mild charge crept across her body (a charge that should have set her hand into motion) and sagged from the tips of her fingers: *Polja is going to die*, and she sensed with bitterness that it was precisely this thought that stayed her limbs, not because she now at long last comprehended that Polja was really not coming with them (she was conscious of that: though Polja would remain alive until two, she would nevertheless not be able to come with them), but rather because she realized that she herself had acquiesced to the fact that Polja would not be going with them.

"Žana," she said, and when she noticed the other woman had moved: "Help me pull Polja's sheet out from under the baby."

"He has more need of it, the baby," Žana said unexpectedly. "And you do too . . . Do you understand . . . ?"—and before Marija could gather her thoughts and say anything, she heard the rustling of the straw and the quiet knocking of the tin can.

"You see, it's too late for that," said Žana. "For Polja, it's too late already."

"What time is it?" Marija asked, at the same time as a narrow blade of light scraped over Žana's face and she saw her lips moving:

"It's not yet midnight. I don't think it's midnight yet."

Marija was just then shifting her frozen legs.

"I got my period," she said. "Or so it seems."

"That's from the fear," Žana said; then she corrected herself: "From the excitement."

"No," Marija said. "From the wet diapers. I didn't dare go to sleep (it was just some kind of half-dozing state). I should have changed position"—then she sensed once more Polja's mute presence in the room (she felt it from the silence) and she remembered that she was supposed to make more diapers out of her sheet. But she didn't get up. She couldn't begin tearing Polja's sheet right away and making diapers. And sanitary pads. Then she asked, "How old was she?" but she already knew that she wasn't going to be able to stand it another second in that position and that her stomach and legs were about to disintegrate abruptly like in Poe's story about the corpse of M. Valdemar, which has been artificially kept alive by means of hypnotism and which then suddenly dissolves into gooey, slimy rot. And even before she could hear Žana's answer, "Seventeen, I think," she had already pushed her hand under the child to extract Polja's sheet, which she then laid next to her on the straw and she laid the child across it and wrapped it up with the other hand. Then she turned to the side for a moment, felt for the edge of the diaper, arched her back, and started unwrapping the wet, blood-covered rags around her legs. "She seemed older to me," she said so that her rubbing the dry edge of a diaper on her benumbed skin to wipe away the blood couldn't be heard.

"Corpses don't have an age," Žana said, and then Marija felt the blood beginning to circulate slowly beneath her skin, rising up through the capillaries to the surface, all over her buttocks and her thighs, and then she stretched out her legs and sat up in the straw, leaning her shoulder blades against the cold wall of the barracks. She wiped her fingers on a damp rag and began groping about in the dark for a dry piece of linen to make a pad.

"You met her before I did," she said, locating her underwear in the gloom beneath the fingers of her right hand, and then she put the folded portion of linen into place between her legs and slid her underwear back up.

"Yes," said Žana. "She was one of those. You know. One of the chosen ones. Along the way she tried to flee. They gave her a thorough beating. Then she got sick and instead of taking her into the *Lebensborn* they dispatched her here. What saved her was the fact that she played the cello. I heard that the overseer who beat her was punished. The Germans regretted that a flower like her should end up on the inside . . ."

Then the straw beneath Žana began to rustle and Marija turned in her direction, following the narrow band of light; she was still lying on her stomach with the straw between her teeth and her eyes fixed on the crack: she was following the movement of the floodlight's beam along the barracks and wire.

The field guns, with their ever-faster salvos in the distance, suddenly fell silent.

"If Polja had lived—" Marija said, and though she wanted to tell the truth: if she had stayed alive till two, in other words until the point at which Maks was going to give the sign, and if she had been left alone in the barracks (since, being so sick, she couldn't go with Žana and Marija)—tomorrow they would have crammed her into a truck anyway and taken her off to the gas chamber, she just couldn't let it end that way for her, so she said: "—she would have been in Odessa in a month or so . . . I believe she was from Odessa"; and Žana said:

"Or maybe if she had just lived a few more hours."

"*They won't take any risks*," Marija said. "That Maks is a damned clever fellow."

"Yes," said Žana. "Damned clever," and then she asked, "Have you ever seen him? Maks, that is?"

"No," Marija said: "Never . . . though actually—" But she couldn't finish her thought, and Marija should have said *We'll get through this* or *We'll make it* or something else just not *They won't take any risks*. And even though she'd stopped with that, and had fallen silent, she began to get clumsily entangled in that heavy net of men, thinking that in terms of needlepoint it was a ridiculous pattern and with the delicate, finely pointed needle of a woman's passivity she began poking into its empty spaces until she found herself wrapped up in the tough, thick threading of the nets and had to call for help from more men, first from Jakob—in her mind—and then, aloud and with desperate entreaty in her voice, that other man too, Maks. The Maks she had still never seen but who had existed for her for months now as a synonym for salvation, the incarnation of masculine god-agency. That's why she'd wanted to say *I've known him as long as I've known Jakob*, but she changed her mind, for she remembered that the true sense of Žana's question lay elsewhere. At least it seemed that way to her. Žana simply wanted to point out that she herself (Marija) wasn't in any condition to do for herself or for her child anything other than submit to the fate that she identified with Jakob, and that that Maks (and she always said "that Maks" herself) was merely the executor of the will of fate-Jakob, and wasn't even a concrete person, with no face and shoulders, no hairy chest and great, powerful hands. Instead: an unknown agent, the hand of God, or the devil himself, or precisely some invisible and unknown powerful third thing that works miracles: he flips some unseen lever or cuts a wire and darkness breaks in . . . Like that night in the corridor when she was coming out of Jakob's room. And before that, too. Ten minutes earlier: all at once the darkness fell. And it was like this:

When Dr. Nietzsche halted in front of Jakob's door he screamed: "These working conditions are impossible! Every five minutes, that power plant! *This smells like sabotage to me,*" and then Jakob covered her mouth so she wouldn't cry out, and then he pushed her, or actually placed her in the cabinet like she was an object and locked her in. But before he shut the door:

"That was Maks," he said. "He shorted out the fuses."

This happened several months ago. Actually more than half a year back. And that was the first time she'd heard of Maks.

3

She sat on Jakob's bed with her legs crossed (blood running down her thighs and along her bottom) and she felt unequal to any new task.

"Jakob, something is going to happen," she said. "I have a feeling that something is going to happen."

And he asked, "What could happen?"

"I don't know," she said. "I just feel like something is going to happen. Maybe someone will find us here"; and then he said:

"Nobody ever comes into my room. Now what would they be looking for in my room?"

"Still, Jakob," she said. "I'm afraid."

But she didn't budge. All she did was say again: "I have a feeling that something could happen," and at that moment she thought about how Aunt Lela had said that this was as important a thing in a woman's life as giving birth, and she thought about the blood she was leaving on Jakob's sheet and about his being a doctor and how he would know what was happening to her. Back then she should have asked Aunt Lela, *Is it possible for it to happen and for the man not to notice anything?*

Then he said: "Should I turn out the light?"; and she:

"No. Stay with me."

"If you're afraid," he said. Then he stopped.

"I'm not," she said. "Only you can't take your hand away." Then more: "I love looking at that lampshade. It's been a year since I saw a lamp with a shade." And again: "I have to go. It's high time I left," but still she did nothing that would indicate she was leaving; made not a single movement that would show that she was leaving. She wasn't capable of making such a motion, although she was no longer lying down (immediately afterward she had stood up and put on her underwear and her dress). Jakob sat at her right side, leaning against the steel frame of the bed. And she just sat there like that, feeling the blood fill up the impression they had made in the straw mattress with their combined weight.

"We've known each other for two months already," she said. "I never could have imagined . . ."

"Who could say," he said. "To me it seems we've known each other for a very long time: for a long while before all this."

"Today's it's exactly eight weeks and a day," she said. "And one night extra. Doesn't that seem like a short time to you . . . ?"

"To me it feels like we've known each other forever," he said. "But never mind that now. This night isn't over yet," and she still couldn't move and she seemed to hear a noise in the corridor and all she could do was cling to him and whisper "Jakob!" and at that same time she realized that he was no longer at her side but somehow here and there by the door listening to the thumping of steps audible right outside, and she felt herself losing the ability to speak on account of fear, and before she could snap out of it and think *This was perhaps my last night with Jakob, my first and last,* before she was in a position to think or say or do anything definite, Jakob was already holding his cupped hand over her mouth. And she was already in the cabinet and realized that its doors were creaking behind her as they closed when she sensed Jakob's face on hers and heard his breathless whisper: "That's Maks," and before she had time to be astonished or at least ask *Maks who?* she nearly simultaneously heard a key start to turn on the outside of the cabinet door and subsequently Jakob's *Ja, ja* and his rapidly receding steps.

Only then did she grasp why she hadn't seen Jakob's face when he said "That's Maks" and that thing about a short-circuit: the light had already been extinguished before he locked the door, for otherwise she would have been able to see Jakob's face; yet she remembered clearly that he hadn't put out the lamp with the shade, and that his tall silhouette had still been visible before her, blocking her light with his back, and then visible too when he turned and bent down and stretched his hand out toward her to cover her mouth and lift her up and deposit her in the cabinet. Now it became clear to her that the light had still been burning when he picked her up and carried her in essentially one swoop, because she remembered seeing a broad swath of wide, dark cracks along the open doors of the cabinet and she understood that he would have to use his foot to fully open those doors that were already ajar. The last thing she saw then was the elongated white stain like some kind of unfleeced animal hanging on a hook, but then right away it struck her that it had to be Jakob's white hospital coat because she could smell the heavy, thick odor of iodoform and ether. So the darkness must have begun at the moment that Jakob's head appeared and touched her face to tell her not to be afraid and to tell her about Maks and the blown circuits, since the cabinet door must have still been open but she nonetheless wasn't able to see him, only to perceive his low, low whisper and his breath on her face.

She stood motionless in the gloom, straining her eyes to pick out some light through the crack along the cabinet's door, and she thought she felt the cabinet vibrating from her suppressed trembling, which the plywood transmitted in every direction, the cabinet shaking and creaking as if it contained a monstrous heart, or else some useless mechanism like a wall clock with no face and no arms with which to carry its weapons: only the frantic, invisible, and pointless click-clack-click-clack of a tremendous pendulum. Her head was at an impossible angle, lying nearly horizontally across the top of her shoulder, but she didn't dare to feel about with her hands in the dark (lest she send an empty clothes hanger flying) or even push that coat farther away, with its sickly sweet hospital smell permeating her eyes and leaving her insides cramped and ready to heave up bile.

But then all she could do was regret that she hadn't taken care of the coat a bit earlier, and she was regretting it all the more when Dr. Nietzsche flipped the switch outside the door to no effect and when, right after that, she caught his voice: "This smells like *sabotage* to me"; she should have done something before that point, at least. Firstly, to move the coat away from her nose (she imagined this movement: sliding the hanger gently along the wooden bar suspended between the two sides of the cabinet, then stopping it with the soft thump of linen on wood, both of these materials springing from plant life, like twins from the same womb, and then her hand making its way back and dropping across her belly

and landing on it with no noise as if it were just returning sound-
lessly through the air and not touching anything at all, and she
imagined her clean, unencumbered breathing and she inhaled the
scent of dry fir planks that radiated the smell of resin); then she
got into a more comfortable position, sitting diagonally or at least
freeing herself from the bar pressing down on her neck. And so it
was as if she were in a coffin: a living corpse; and she thought of
Anijela. She would always remember: the elliptical tin sign on a
flaking red facade, COFFINS MADE HERE—THROUGH THE
ARCH, LEFT—hidden in the summer by the leaves of the wild
chestnuts and with the gnarled, clumsily painted finger pointing
like the hand of fate in the direction of the graves; THROUGH
THE ARCH, LEFT under the blooming boughs of the wild chestnut; and she thought back to the heavy aromatic smell of chestnut
blossoms and to that cul-de-sac straying off of Grobljanska Street
and then going left. Now she could also remember the ice-flowers
on the window between which appeared the head of the gray-
haired old man inside like the head of some faun among the ferns,
and she recalled his mouth of crooked and missing teeth below his
big mustache, and when their round faces filled the opaque flowers of his window he exhaled on it to melt the ice. Then, under his
reeking breath, the fern withered, and Aunt Lela pulled the scarf
away from her face so that he would recognize her: "It's us, Čika
Martin"; then a flickering yellow light came on in the window and
after that one could hear the key turning in the lock and she saw
the faun's disheveled head and mustache and immediately she regretted coming, even before the man said: "This one's not coming
to me for a place to stay, is she?" But Aunt Lela said:

"No. She's not. She just came by to see Anijela. How is Anijela?"

27

They stood in the corner of his darkened workshop and warmed up by the low fire smoldering in a round sawdust-fed stove. Two or three times the man lifted the lid and peered in at the embers, each time spitting into the fire and then sticking his pipe back in his mouth. But she had still not seen Anijela. They were waiting until they had warmed up a bit, but Marija had already firmly decided that she would not be staying, whatever happened. It wasn't precisely on account of the old man but much more because of the low ceiling, smoky and peeling, and due to the sense that death had permeated everything here; she almost couldn't look at that black gilt-edged coffin lid standing upright by the door.

"She sleeps all the time," the old man said. He took the pipe out of his mouth. Then with his middle finger he tamped down the bowl and she saw that the stunted index finger on his right hand was fastened to his middle finger like some sort of parasite. "I tell her it would be better for her to get some exercise," he said. "It's impossible for anybody to come in here without my hearing them first. But she doesn't want to get up until *it passes*, as she says. *All this must pass.*"

Marija saw Anijela right after that, as they were moving between the workshop and the warehouse. She remembered: the old man latched the door of the workshop, then he took a candle and set off in front of them. She had to walk on for a bit before she grew accustomed to the half-darkness (the man was shielding his candle) and was able to orient herself: coffins, for the most part unpainted, lay diagonally on the shelves like beds on some kind of ship of the dead. She took in the dense, heavy smell of glue, fresh logs, and planks of fir, oil paints, and turpentine.

Then the man repeated:

"You see? I told you. She's sleeping again," and he raised the lid from one of the caskets in the corner of the room. "All she does is sleep. In the evenings she comes out, but only to go to one place—you know what I mean. Then she comes right back." Then he told her: "She has feathers in there. And the chimney runs along beside her there. She's not cold, she says."

Just then Marija caught sight of Anijela, who slowly raised her eyelids, and then only the whites of her eyes showed, and these words came dragging out of her mouth:

"I'm always sleepy," Anijela said. "As soon as I let the lid down, I fall asleep." Her eyes were twitching as if the meager illumination of the candle were blinding her.

At that point, the man said, "That's from the dust. It would be better for her if she took a shot of rakija. That'd invigorate her, as I say. And give her some courage."

"No," Anijela responded. "The dust helps me sleep"; then she looked at Marija, as if speaking only to her: "I have the same dream over and over: someone is after me and I can't run away. Then I wake up and see that I'm in a coffin. So I calm down a little. Do you ever dream anything like this, Marija? Someone is chasing you, and you . . ."

Then Aunt Lela came to her assistance:

"Sweetheart," she said, "how about you come out of that . . . out of there. We'll try to get you a passport. Or something." Then she added, "Later on, of course. When things have calmed down, a little bit at least."

"Oh, no," said the doll-sleeper. "I'll wait right here for the end of the war. I like it fine here. Really. This is great for me, Aunt Lela"; and Marija, astonished, disbelieving, looked at her face and her pale eyes: her head shrunken as with those prizes prepared by headhunters, no bigger than a fist; her mouth splitting her face in half, unchanged and so disproportionate in relation to her narrow, knotty nose and the delicate wax lines embossed on the doll-sleeper's miniature face. Even her eyelashes were of a supernatural length and fell and rose with a sound like the scraping, loud and ungreased, of the wings of a night bird. Then Marija's eyes stopped on Anijela's necklace with its chunky artificial beads the color of amethyst; that necklace on the slender neck of the doll-sleeper gave Anijela the look of those mummies found in the pyramids of the Pharaohs: the dignity of a ruler's death.

"That's from my late mother," Anijela said abruptly, before Marija could inquire about the significance of the necklace and before she could think of anything at all to say, at least anything other than what you would say to someone on their deathbed; "a family heirloom, as they say," Anijela went on as if responding to Marija's unspoken question and to her look that had now turned into a wild if suppressed cry. But then her eyes stopped on Anijela's scrawny, withered fingers, with which she was picking at her necklace as if counting on her rosary; she still had long, well-groomed nails the color of dark silver that somehow, miraculously, matched the bleached-out amber of those long fingers, like a silver crown on the elegant, old-fashioned tube of a precious cigarette-holder.

"I use it as a calendar," she said. "If each bead stands for one month, then there is more than three years' worth here. I guess the war will be over by then. But a bead can also stand for a week. Or a day. Or an hour." And she repeated: "I'm counting"; and Marija

felt that she wouldn't be able to say a word and that she would
have to wait for the old man to put down his pipe for a moment
or to mumble something, would have to wait for anything, and
anything would do, so long as someone said something and she
didn't have to listen to Anijela's hoarse whisper anymore, so long
as someone said something in a human voice, even for the old
man to clear his throat in deep bass tones, or for Aunt Lela, in
her manly voice, reeking of cigarettes, to say something pointless
or implausible, like that line a little while earlier about a passport
for Anijela; but instead of any of that Marija was again forced to
hear the whispering of the doll-sleeper: "And when I'm bored I
play it a lot," the mummy said, and her fingers the color of dark
amber flew over the necklace, stopping for an instant when they
seemed to have found the right note and chord, unregistered by
her audience but that showed in her eyes across which scurried
the skittish shadows of some unearthly melody (and now she remembered Polja's figure wrapped around the rising neck of a cello
beneath the black canopy of that hearse parked near the crematorium while dark rain trickled from the sky as they were returning
to work, soaking wet and fatigued): "So there," Anijela said then
and moved her head back a little so that the point of her chin pro-
truded upward as in those paintings of the descent from the Cross
with their impossibly foreshortened perspective in which his toes,
the hollow beneath his ribs, and his triangular chin align; "Tram-
tram-tram-tram," Anijela conveyed to them the sounds that were
crashing around in her mind but remained inaudible to them, all
the while tapping her fingers on those glass beads the color of amethyst: "Mozart," she said as if breathing out the word in a pause of

a sixteenth note's duration or between two half notes: "*Requiem*," she said, without stopping her delirious finger movements, her head suspended over the imaginary piano: "I even know when I'm doing it wrong. I know exactly which note is which and as soon as I hit one I can hear it perfectly."

And Marija had already opened her mouth to tell Aunt Lela that they had to go because she could no longer stand to listen to Anijela's *Requiem*, but then the emergency sirens went off somewhere and took her breath away, but at that moment she would have preferred to hear the hysterical howling of a siren to Anijela's whispering, and in the same moment she realized that they would have to stay for at least fifteen minutes more until the alarm passed. Fortunately Anijela fell asleep all of a sudden, as if lulled by her own music, and they, the three of them, that is to say Aunt Lela, the old man, and she, could talk about something in the indirect and silly way people usually talk; then the old man said that his common sense told him the war couldn't last longer than a year because at that point God would either have taken pity on people or have destroyed the whole world with fire and flood, because he knew an old man in their area who up to now had prophesied about several wars and that included the exact day and month and year and he had even predicted the assassination in Sarajevo and had spoken about it in plain terms to everyone and for that reason he was thrown in prison and after it actually happened the way he had prognosticated (in the same way that he had prophesied about several droughts and even the date of birth and name of the heir to the throne) they let him go but first he had to tell them where he had obtained his knowledge of it and he let them know it was all written down, nice and tidy, in the Old Testament and in various books of prophecy; well, it's this same old fellow who said this too, that this war cannot last for very long because how could it come to pass that people would hurl themselves into trenches this way like animals and pile up in heaps two dozen at a time and he remembered well what it had been like when he'd fought in a war under Emperor Franz Josef—but Marija was no longer listening to him she was already concentrating on this visit having to be over at some point and she was waiting for the siren to give the signal that the alarm was over and as she did that she looked into the candle so that she didn't have to look into Anijela's coffin anymore. Then after an eternity the siren screeched again and Aunt Lela said, "We don't want to wake her. Let her rest"; and that was all Marija had been waiting for: by the time the old man closed the lid on Anijela's coffin she was already in the next room and even all the way outside, where she had fled to escape herself and everything else, and then the man said:

"It wouldn't be a bad thing for her to take a little rakija. It's better than dust," and Aunt Lela:

"To be sure. To be sure"; but Marija was already standing in the threshold by the door and staring into the clean, newly fallen snow as though at a miracle. Meanwhile now she was still standing, immobile, with her back squeezed up against the rod in the cabinet and with her head practically jammed into that stinking hospital coat until with one of her hands she pressed on her underwear and felt the blood coat her fingers and run down her leg, and she had the impression that she was going to bleed out like a butchered animal hanging from a hook, head down in a slaughterhouse while blood slowly drips and congeals on the concrete down below in a thick scarlet stain. It was obvious to her: she could do nothing; she would have to remain standing in this impossible position until something happened, until Dr. Nietzsche left or Jakob tried something; all she had to do was see to it that she didn't pass out because to do so would betray her presence, and that she go on waiting there, her teeth clenched. She had already heard the doctor's deep harsh voice that sometimes ended sentences in an unpleasant and unexpected *falsetto* and suddenly she realized that the light was burning again outside and that, therefore, the blown fuses had been fixed, for along the cabinet's door a sharp fissure of light had appeared. *That Maks had again managed to get away with it*, she thought, and at the same time she heard Jakob's voice too.

"He's gotten us out of a lot of tight spots," Marija said after a brief pause: she said *us* because that word also means "you," meaning Žana, because it was clear that the preparations for their escape were in large part Maks's work; he was there in the background; he pulled unseen strings; he created light and engineered blown circuits. He. Maks. Whom no one saw.

Then she heard Žana's voice in an echo of a sentence spoken just before:

"Damned clever fellow," and Marija thought that this was the only way Jakob would ever be able to compliment another man. Not that Žana had any such difficulties. But her "Damned clever fellow" was welcome nonetheless. And Marija imagined telling Žana about what came after, when Dr. Nietzsche finally departed and she said good-bye to Jakob and headed toward the barracks door, at the end of the hallway; and then she thought *It would be better if I tried to sleep a bit. I need to be rested.* And she pressed the child to her and said in a whisper, without turning her head:

"I have the impression that time is passing more slowly than ever. I think it would still be the best thing for me to sleep a bit. Especially if it's past midnight."

4

And although she wasn't able to sleep, she was also not in a position to tell Žana what happened later, not only because she was upset and afraid but also because she was preoccupied with herself to such an extent that she was hardly able to think in chronological terms and she hardly knew what came before and what afterward, and it was as if all kinds of time had flowed into one, and it was also because it seemed impossible to her to separate from the whole web of occurrences one single story like the one about Maks, nearly indistinguishable from the shapeless mass of achronicity out of which her mind now selected things in no apparent order. So she was fully in the grip of all this, and she wouldn't have been able to tell Žana even if she'd wanted to, or even tell herself, what happened later.

But she could still hear the doctor's voice and she tried to make sense of the sequence: first she heard the scraping of the chair on the floor, and then the chair creaked under its load (and she understood that Dr. Nietzsche had lowered his weight onto the chair and she immediately thought that something was wrong here if a Dr. Nietzsche, also known as the Nazi Hippocrates, a highly regarded researcher with "human guinea pigs" and a highly placed secret advisor on racial questions, if, therefore, a person like that arrives unannounced and without escort and what's more at that time of night at a subordinate's room, the room of a non-Aryan colleague—according to his own (Dr. Nietzsche's) racial theory), and she began to recount to herself everything Jakob had told her about that man who supervised the crematorium and the "Institute for Scientific Research." And even without all that, even if she hadn't known of Dr. Nietzsche and if Jakob hadn't talked to her about him, the former professor of anatomy at the University of Strasbourg, she would have grasped that something wasn't right when a German doctor paid a visit to Jakob and did so at that time of night; she knew that something unusual was occurring as soon as the chair groaned and even before the doctor inquired of Jakob in an almost confidential tone:

"Are you alone?"

"Yes," said Jakob. "Of course. Who would be here at this time of day?"

"For example, one of those women whom you saved from the camp and took for your own."

"That would be the same as there being no one here. They're only guinea pigs."

"Never mind that now," Dr. Nietzsche said. "I'm here on a confidential matter." Then he paused before saying:

"We consider you a trustworthy person."

"I'm only a doctor," Jakob replied.

"Do you really mean *only a doctor*?" asked Dr. Nietzsche, "or do you mean *a trustworthy doctor*?—I guess you've thought about that."

"Yes," Jakob said. "As has every doctor. I think of my professional oath, Herr Nietzsche: I will endeavor to justify the *trust* that my patient has in me."

"And have you, Herr Doktor, justified that trust? Always?"

"Yes," Jakob said.

"And you have always done for your patients everything that *lay within your powers*?"

"I believe I have," Jakob said again. "Within the limits of my powers."

"And how many of your patients have died?—I mean from among those who trusted you?"

"No one trusts anyone anymore," Jakob answered.

"You didn't answer my question, Herr Doktor. How many of them have died?"

"I don't remember," Jakob said. "Many of them . . . though I don't think it was through any fault of mine." Then he added: "Many of them were killed."

"You mean at headquarters and in the gas chambers?"

"Yes," said Jakob. "In those places also, of course."

She was already anticipating the turn the conversation would now take, following all that Jakob had said.

"*Have you ever considered, my dear colleague, trying it out yourself? Having a look at all this from the inside*?" Dr. Nietzsche asked. "Maybe it would interest you to inquire personally about the degree to which the gas chamber is more humane than, let's say, the guillotine. Or the hangman's rope. Don't forget: *there is still time for everything.*"

"I know," Jakob replied. "Whenever I'm about to forget that, even for a moment—" (but he didn't finish, and she was certain that she would now give herself away with some desperate movement meaning "*No, Jakob, don't go on!*" or that she would collapse

38

unconscious or otherwise announce her presence from the cabinet against her will like a broken wall clock when all of a sudden it begins to clang before one of the mechanisms snaps and it finally falls silent . . . but nothing happened. Even Dr. Nietzsche didn't demand that Jakob finish what he had started but instead, as if he were saving him, he brought down the blade of his axe before Jakob's head could reach the chopping block):

"Let us imagine," said Dr. Nietzsche, interrupting, "that someone orders you to carry out a certain experiment on a group of prisoners who, you have been told or have found out some other way, are going to be killed anyway," after which there was a slight pause, "would you not feel that there was a certain *professional*, scientific gain in that? Being able to conduct observations of living beings, of human beings, actually? At any rate, you'd have to admit that every experiment has human testing as its ultimate goal."

"Perhaps," Jakob said, "assuming I had their agreement. Perhaps then . . . under certain circumstances."

"What do you mean?" Dr. Nietzsche asked.

Jakob didn't answer right away. Then he said:

"Let us say that I consider these experiments . . . reasonable. Not merely useful from a professional, scientific point of view. Let's assume . . . "

"But," Dr. Nietzsche interrupted again, and Marija managed to tear herself away from the conversation long enough to reflect that she now understood almost nothing of this situation and that she couldn't fathom where this whole discussion was leading, although from the fear that was constricting her throat she sensed that Jakob wanted to add something to his "Let's assume" that

would be dangerous for him in the extreme, and therefore dangerous for her—but at the moment she heard Dr. Nietzsche's voice interrupting Jakob's she could only think how she understood nothing of what their two voices were saying, and she imagined the
two of them facing off against each other in the darkness that was
for her impenetrable and blotted out all distinctions and she per-
ceived them only as half-whispers painting the invisible speakers
with expressions of tense, concealed attentiveness; now Nietzsche's
tense and rushed whisper had the floor once more, and now the
two of them—in their unseen combat—more readily resembled
conspirators hatching some plan than what she knew them to be:
enemies, separated by opposing convictions and prejudices about
race and ideology and power and every other possible and impossible difference, but who for a moment were accepting (illusorily
at least) points of view that were in essence the opposites of their
own so that in this way, by means of that ostensible identification,
they could each prove to the other that their adversarial stand-
points were in fact shared; even though they were both likewise
convinced that such duplicity was in fact one of the easiest ways
to allow their own convictions to come into view. Of course, that
ostensible identification was doomed: this was a game of poker
between a king and one of his subjects, in which the king would
allow himself to lose only by virtue of his mercy so long as he
found some form of satisfaction in competing on an equal footing
with his people: ultimately he must emerge as the winner because
he's holding three kings in his hand; the subject displays his hand
with a triumphant smile and starts to slide the whole of the state
exchequer toward himself when the king gives a sign to his armed

guards: *Stop. Here are three kings, and I make—four.* And smiling bitterly the subject gives back the money to which he had added everything he still possessed and he laughs along with the others at the king's deceit and applauds his wit, and then he steps out and fires a bullet into his own mouth in front of the palace gates as a symbol of protest: that is as much as Marija comprehended of the proceedings when Dr. Nietzsche resumed playing and she heard the continuation of that word "But":

". . . no one is asking you if you consider it reasonable or useful or whatever else you want to call it. *You have simply been handed an order—a command*—to conduct certain experiments on people, even though they might seem mad or absurd to you. It's the same as when a noncommissioned officer is issued some order (and in our case it is in fact an instance of an order of a military nature) and he is not allowed to consider and does not need to understand why he and his squad have to defend the approaches to a certain bridge. He will *perish defending* those approaches, along with his entire squad, without considering the context or any potential personal doubts about the appropriateness of the mission or this tactical maneuver.—It's the same in a doctor's case when he's been ordered to carry out (let us say) the complete sterilization of a certain group or even a race or to put into effect a program of euthanasia or of tests with vaccines or low temperatures: when that doctor refuses to execute the trials as ordered by the official institution in command it is assured that he will be called to account for this disobedience. *In such a case—and here one must also consider the authoritarian character of our state—an individual's adherence to the ethical code of a given profession has to yield to the total nature of this war*"; and from out of his meaty, round palm, squeezed into a jagged fist that was banging gingerly on the table, flew a stupid jack of spades in a green corporal's tunic.

Jakob cast his experienced gambler's eye over that card, over the Prussian figure in its tunic, with its two symmetrical bodies and two symmetrical swords as in a mirror and suddenly that mirror-doubled figure struck him as simultaneously dangerous and ludicrous; although she couldn't see the expression on his face, or his legs under the table, or even hear his breathing or anything else by which she could gain an insight into Jakob's condition, she was *a priori* convinced that he would not take any more risks now, if for no other reason than because of her, for he had to be thinking of her the entire time, Marija trembling in the cabinet, on the verge of unconsciousness, participating in this dangerous game not only as a kibitzer behind Jakob's back but also as an unseen fellow player, a silent partner, a camouflaged prompter who wouldn't permit him to get in over his head and who reined in the passion of the game in the name of weakness and in the name of a fear that Jakob must have sensed when he added unconvincingly (to her, anyway) and placatingly (to Dr. Nietzsche):

"I don't know. It's hard to understand all this, to make sense of everything," and Marija remembered having asked Jakob to do something for Marija Beljanska, her namesake, who was at one time bunking in the same barracks as her: she had been summoned, along with a group of ten other women, and told to report to Dr. Nietzsche, and he had given them some injections that caused their legs to swell up; several times Marija underwent an operation in which she couldn't see what they were doing with her leg, which hurt terribly and was wrapped up and put in a cast. Later they took off the bandages and plaster, and pus came trickling out of the wound. She was unable to stand on that leg. And then, immediately thereafter, they led her away to the gas chamber; but before that she had asked Jakob for help, right at the start: and she still remembered the look on his face and his voice:

Those are Dr. Nietzsche's experiments.

What's that supposed to mean, Jakob?

Someone should slip her some morphine. Or something like that. Do you see?

So that she'll die?

Yes. So she'll go to sleep; then she understood everything and she recalled Marija's mood when she had been summoned the first time: she believed that after the examination she would be packed off home. So she told Jakob once more:

Do that for her. Try to do it for her. I implore you, Jakob.

I'll try, Jakob said. *But it should have been done earlier. I worry that it's already too late.*

She knew, therefore, that Jakob wasn't going to protest now but also wasn't going to be lulled into complacency; and anyway it was high time for Dr. Nietzsche to start whatever he had come to Jakob for at that time of night, the real conversation he wanted to have, just between them, a confidential talk, as though between colleagues; that is, that thing on account of which he had right till this moment been hemming and hawing and mincing around Jakob with his little short sword, but in a conciliatory way, as if he were only playing, though Jakob had to feel the danger too, or else he wouldn't have said, a little earlier, "If I were to forget

43

that even for a minute . . ." a comment he didn't finish although it had to mean something, but Dr. Nietzsche would have to get to the point at last if for no other reason than because Jakob would challenge him eventually for he surely hadn't forgotten that he'd locked Marija in the cabinet, and he knew that she couldn't stand there like that forever but was going to collapse or cry out or give a loud moan; and then she thought that maybe it was a good thing that she too—even though it came at the cost of so great an effort and so many trials—was in attendance at this secret duel, this dangerous game in which one of the players has a jack of spades with two swords on his side and the other has only the imaginary shield of a poker face and his intellect and perhaps of time as well: if the Allied forces somewhere in Europe or in the Urals or the Pacific didn't manage to remove several tens of thousands of jacks of clubs, clad in tunics and armed with their two swords, from the deck, and soon, thereby joining forces with time (the ace of hearts), Dr. Nietzsche would have his two SS men work Jakob over—in spades—as punishment for his disobedience and his passive resistance, and Marija would remain there in that cabinet bleeding out like a slaughtered lamb hung upside down on a hook. And for an instant she wondered how this game without rules would evolve if she weren't there; she decided that even if she bled to death and so stopped eavesdropping and spying on the game, invisible but present, even then they would, nonetheless, still feel her mute presence (in the same way that she now felt the presence of Polja's corpse in the barracks), her testimony or her accusation: Jakob would then, if only that one time, give a different response, even though it might only vary by a shade from the one he threw back at Dr. Nietzsche now, in front of her.

The chair scraped anew and she saw the unseen skull of Dr. Nietzsche and his graying locks *á la* Schopenhauer, as she had noted to herself the first time she saw him, as he looked angrily into Jakob's invisible face:

"You are familiar with the situation on the front lines?" he said.

"One hears talk."

"Unfortunately, it's accurate," Dr. Nietzsche said. "The Allies are advancing. You know that to be the case. No less so than I do."

"It's more that I have a premonition of it," Jakob said.

"Yes, yes. You're all . . . You're all Bergsonians, goddamn it." He paused for a moment: "Intuition . . . versus free will."

"Ah," Jakob continued. "*Also sprach Zarathustra.*"

"Never mind that now," Dr. Nietzsche said nervously. "Let's get down to cases; this conversation has led us far afield."

Then, at last, he said something which must have signified the beginning of that discussion for the sake of which he was now sitting there with Jakob—she was just as impatient as either of the men—so that things could finally get started and then what had to happen could finally happen and this game could be wrapped up and she could be rescued but it still seemed to her that time wasn't moving, was at a standstill, just like this conversation being conducted by two voices, their speakers invisible, while she bled to the point of passing out with strained attentiveness in a position of both disfigured sacrifice and unseen witness; she was horribly dependent upon the words and the voices she could hear and on the facial expressions and hand gestures she couldn't see while at the same time aware of her own role and her own movements, her own immobility that was every bit as significant and momentous as the two men's words; aware to the point of pain

and numbness both that every movement of her hand and even every beat of her pulse was governed by that diminutive cogwheel of events; and not only that: even every one of her thoughts connected with Jakob denoted something essential because it guided her and floated, invisibly present, now more than ever before, because of that sacrificial blood that was running out of her and depriving her of strength and dimming her consciousness—it was not just the pledge of her absolute union with Jakob but also the pledge and guarantee of her complicity in all of life's temptations and accordingly also the pledge and guarantee of their joint conspiracy against death, and accordingly she had to hold out and not pass out, especially now, when it had already commenced, the thing to which she was so insanely bearing witness with her presence and her blood that was not merely the price of love and of love's embrace but also (miraculously) evidence of the principle of life and of the thirst for life, for the presence or appearance of death always challenges love to pair off with it and mate so that finally one of them can take up the conqueror's standard and wave it above the world; that breathless pairing of corpses and that love between Eros and Thanatos, born of antagonism, was no less than the clash of fundamental elements, of earth and blood, sometimes nearly incomprehensible as long as one is thinking of the basic nature of those substances and their original components: the vague, well-nigh organic sensation of all of this kept her mind alert; this encounter between love and death in her consciousness and in her blood: she could still hear Dr. Nietzsche's words, uttered in a lowered voice, in what was almost a whisper: "*I have a concrete suggestion for you* ... More or less a *quid pro quo*. Yes. A little favor in return."

"A favor in return?" Jakob asked.

"A trifle," Nietzsche responded. "You will do a little job for me. If you don't deny that it is only your doing me a favor in return . . . . But of course. Only in that case. Otherwise . . ."

"Otherwise what?" Jakob asked. "Otherwise what?"

"Otherwise I can remind you of the favors I've already done you. By way of the fact that you're still alive, for one . . . But I don't believe you would show me such ingratitude. I don't believe you would walk away just like that. Without a rematch." And then the doctor went on, still bearing arms, albeit merely a wooden, gold-plated sword: "But it's still too soon for good-byes. I think it is too soon indeed . . . so let me get to the point."

"I'm listening," Jakob said; then Dr. Nietzsche:

"I'm talking to you above all as a scientist and a doctor. Bear that in mind. As a *Nazi doctor*, of course."

"But of course," Jakob said. "I'm listening."

"You know about the collecting of Jewish skulls and skeletons?"

"I've heard about it."

"So much the better. I had assumed as much; it means at the very least that you've already thought about all of this," Dr. N. said, ". . . and that you have, naturally, your own opinions about it all."

"Actually . . . " but Jakob couldn't finish his sentence.

"At this time I have no intention (after all I've just told you) of inquiring after your personal opinion on the matter. I only want to remind you that the bottom line is that that these collections number among the favors that I mentioned to you a moment ago (to your prodigious amazement), which I undertook on your behalf . . ."

"For me?"

"For your nation," Nietzsche said. "Same thing." Then he corrected himself: "For your *race*, actually."

"I don't understand," Jakob said. "For my race . . . ?"

"It amazes me the way your intuition . . . But let's drop it for now.—It is, I believe, obvious to you that should genocide be carried out (as has been planned—something you also know full well), nothing would remain of your race except this collection of skulls."

"It's not clear to me—" Jakob said, "I'm not completely clear on what it is you want from me. Even if I could intuit what you're getting at with this talk of *favors* you've done for my race, as you put it, it remains unclear to me what my return favor should, in concrete terms, consist of."

"Simple," Dr. Nietzsche said in confidence. "I want you to do whatever you can to keep the collection from being destroyed, *if this becomes necessary*. I think you understand me. It is especially important (and this is part of your assignment) that your rescue only be attempted . . ." Then he stopped, looking for the right word: ". . . *at the right time*. Yes. At the right time. I think you understand me. I am speaking in the interests of science more than anything (which in this case are also the interests of your race): *Do not allow this collection to be destroyed*."

"I don't understand," Jakob said. "I truly do not understand."

"This means nothing to you?" Dr. Nietzsche asked, almost offended.

"That's not the point," Jakob said. "I simply don't understand what my assignment actually consists of—nor my favor in return."

"Well then," Dr. Nietzsche continued, after a brief, strained silence: "I will have to leave the matter up to you. It's up to you to

convince yourself that I am not in a position to act contrary to an order even when my *personal* opinion runs *contrary* to *it*. Or if I have individual *scientific* reasons to disobey."

And so Doctor Nietzsche was now breathing rapidly and sounded asthmatic:

"*From the highest level,*" he said as if he were speaking the first lines of *Genesis*. "From the highest level we have received orders for all traces of our experiments, including the collecting of Jewish skulls and skeletons, to be destroyed. Not yet, of course, but as soon as it proves necessary"; he was gaining momentum: "Well, so now I too am delivered into your hands . . . Do you know what they call what I just told you?—*Treason!*" His pathetic whisper continued: "Betrayal of military secrets at the highest level . . . As you can see, we're not talking here about adherence or non-adherence to professional ethical principles but about military, *wartime accountability*. I am telling you this only because I want once more to underscore the delicacy of the situation and the untenability of my own individual initiative . . . "

"In concrete terms, wherein does *my* individual initiative lie?" Jakob asked. "In my violation of a direct order from Himmler?"

"*C'est ça,*" Nietzsche said. ". . . In the interests of science. And (perhaps, in the event that the wind begins to blow in our favor again) also of your race. There isn't a Nazi anywhere who would do this: it contravenes, you know . . . contravenes our conception of autocracy."

"All right," Jakob said. "What is it that I have to do?"

"You have to wait," Nietzsche replied. "And to keep quiet . . . For now, that's it."

"And after that . . . "

"Providing that it becomes apparent to you that our side has completely collapsed, the German side—you know exactly what I mean—and if I am absent from the scene (and you should assume this will be the case), then there is nothing for you to do, and there is no need for you to prevent anyone from doing what he will with the collections." Then, after a short pause in which he took another breath, he continued with pathos: "But if it seems to you—according to your own findings—that the time for that has still not come, *then endeavor to prevent the destruction of these valuable collections* that could wind up being the only remaining evidence of your extinct race."

Nearly twenty-four hours would have to pass before Jakob could explain to Marija the meaning of this whole tragicomedy, titled "The Fanatic: or, in the Service of Science," because Dr. Nietzsche wanted, as Jakob said, to have in him (that is, in Jakob) a reliable witness in case he should one day fall into the hands of the Allies, a likelihood that he'd now had time to think through. But it was not as *the strange case of Dr. Nietzsche* that all this mattered to her; rather, the experience was for her a sign and an omen, because, as Jakob said, something serious had happened; but Jakob expressed at the same time the fear that the Germans prior to evacuating would indeed destroy every trace of the camp so that one day they could stand before the Eyes of History, innocently shrugging their shoulders, and so that same evening (the very day after Nietzsche's nocturnal visit), Jakob said for the first time:

"*We must try to prevent this.*" Then he added what she in slightly modified form had told Žana earlier, in a distant echo of this same sentence of Jakob's uttered nearly a year earlier: "*But we cannot put anything at risk. Now is a very bad time to die.*"

5

When Dr. Nietzsche finally said *Perhaps it was too early for this visit* and stood up from his chair, she thought: *At last*, because it seemed to her that if he stayed a minute longer she would have given herself away, probably by passing out. Then she heard the rustling of straw from the bed, from which she could conclude that Jakob had already stood up, and then his footsteps, the key in the door, Nietzsche's conspiratorial and practically confiden-tial *Auf Wiedersehen!* and she sensed her legs abruptly giving way beneath her as she slipped down the wardrobe: the last thing she felt was a sharp pain in her shoulder blades as she slid down the plank, and then there was a dull thud and, after that, darkness . . .

"Jakob," she said, and that was the first thing that sprouted in her mind, with a weak flash, amid the crimson swirls, growing brighter and brighter, and then it was between her lips. Then those swirls started to expand in concentric circles and in the emerging gap she could make out Jakob's face, bent over her, and she could feel his hand on her forehead. "Take that away, Jakob," she said and with the same effort that it took to speak those words she raised her arm and pushed aside the little bottle of ammonia that Jakob was holding beneath her nose. And without turning her

head she gathered that the light brightening Jakob's face was located somewhere to the side, on the floor: *Jakob's placed the lamp with the shade on the floor*, she thought all of a sudden, and she remembered everything that had happened and she clasped her arms around Jakob's neck. He lifted her up and put her on the bed and returned the lamp with the shade to the table by the bed.

"How long was I unconscious?" she asked.

"I don't know," he said. "As soon as I locked the door, I raced back to the wardrobe. I realized immediately that something wasn't right. I reached in my pocket for the key but couldn't find it. Then I drummed my nails on the door of the cabinet, even though I sensed that something had happened to you. At the same time I recalled hiding the key under my pillow. I grabbed it along with the bottle of ammonia on the table and, wouldn't you know it, I found you sitting on the floor of the wardrobe with your head tilted over onto your shoulder . . . I heard nothing at all when you fell," he said . . . "Poor thing"; and as he caressed her she thought that Jakob must know everything now, because he has to have seen the blood and thus he knows that she is his wife, even if he hadn't noticed anything earlier; otherwise why would he have said "You poor thing." And then she said:

"I fell right as he was leaving." Then, with the concealed pride of being Jakob's wife: "I couldn't go on. I couldn't hold out a single minute longer. Your coat did me in. *I don't know how I can love a man whose coat reeks like this. I will have to find another man.*"

Then he said:

"*I don't know how I can love a woman who passes out so easily. I will have to find another woman*"; his palms lingered gently on her

cheeks. In that moment of forgetfulness her thoughts temporarily swung in the opposite direction, with her eyes now immobile and concentrated on that one single point of focus where Jakob was to be found. She (Jakob's wife) all of a sudden started to expand and evaporate; the red-hot focal point began to cool off as soon as—having long since learned to take slaps like this in stride—her consciousness began to take in her surroundings: the lamp with the shade—Jakob's room—window blocked with a blanket—and beyond the window: damp gelid night, pierced by spotlights and barbed wire. The concentric circles then started to radiate through the night, into space and time, grazing the dim border between future and past, and when she quickly and fearfully and force-fully halted the waves being emitted by her mind and when they returned from the obscure and distant stretches of the night to Jakob's room, to the two of them, all she found was a black, singed hole in her mind, there where, a short time before, there had been the hot focal point of the lamp with the apple-blossom lampshade; now in that place was that unhinged voice once again, a voice that sometimes ended sentences in a falsetto and which was known as "Dr. Nietzsche" . . .

"I don't get it," she said. "I don't understand what that guy wanted from you."

"Covering his retreat," Jakob told her. "What else would he be trying to do: *protecting his escape route.* Understand?"

"Not really," she said. "It still isn't completely clear in my mind . . . Is he not able to do all of that himself? Isn't there anyone else he could order around, anyone else he trusts more? It doesn't quite make sense . . . Tell me, Jakob: *Is this really it?*"

Jakob reflected for a moment.

"Judging by all this—yes," he said. "By this comedy . . ." (Then he told her the real meaning of Nietzsche's visit; it gave her a modicum of hope, and in the quantity necessary for fear not to take the day.)

She remembered: Jakob had told her then: Yes, *judging by all this*, and although there was doubt in his voice (at least it seemed that way to her), she nonetheless sensed a flash of hope in him and she sensed too that what was in his voice was only bitterness and not despair; and hope too of course. And more. Just now was the first time that Jakob had added, definitively if a little bit mistrustfully, "Judging by all this." But he did not say: "Hope is a necessity. Thus we have to imagine it," nor that other thing he added at the beginning: "Otherwise you won't be able to hold out for one day in this camp. Without hope it would be as if a person were to break ranks and announce to everyone, to their faces, that they were doomed. Each and every one. Things couldn't go on like that for even a single day. You have to live. Only the person without hope is a real corpse. Do you understand? That's why you can't abandon hope. Even if it flees, finding no room in your heart . . . Lure it back. Thaw it out. Revive it with artificial resuscitation, by trickery, or even by force . . ." But that had been right at the beginning, a day or two after they'd first met; she remembered: at that time she didn't completely believe him; and alongside all the sincerity that resonated in his words, still it seemed to her that he said what he said out of self-confidence or out of cowardice and those both struck her as being pointless at that moment. Maybe he's just some devious collaborator, or just a frightened one. Back then she hadn't known him as well as she would. She'd only seen him one time before that. When she was arriving at the camp. Therefore she had said to him that second time, before she got to know him and while she still doubted him:

"Do you think, Doctor, that I can bother with something like hope here and now, in Auschwitz?" And she amazed herself with the trust in him that her voice then betrayed: "That at this very moment I can tap into the reserve of hope people carry in their hearts?"

"I don't doubt it," he said. "You've certainly suffered a great deal up to this point. But have you really lost hope?" She had no answer for him, despite the trust she'd begun to feel for him; she truly didn't know how to respond, for who knows what's going on in this game with no rules, "I hope/I have no hope," like "I will/I won't" or "He loves me/He loves me not," because it was somehow always like this, both in the train car when they were being deported and on the way to the camp and earlier as well, on the Danube: she accepted it, and to her it seemed like she was reconciling herself to all that was coming her way, but later she realized that she had actually not acquiesced completely and that she hadn't ever abandoned altogether a certain madness that could be called hope (perhaps not even then, at the Danube; but she was in no position now to be certain of that); thus she wanted to say to him that maybe none of it had anything to do with hope, for she had managed to stay alive that time by the Danube, back when it all started (it was three or four years ago), and instead maybe it was all nothing more than an absurd game without rules, a game in which it was impossible to stake anything, even hope, and she wanted to tell him the story of what happened back then by the

Danube as she waited at the green peeling fence much as she used to stand in line for a shower during a summer heat wave; but she remembered that she hadn't abandoned that insanity, which could also be called hope, she hadn't abandoned it even then all the way up to the point at which she lost consciousness; but her eyes would shut—even then (leaving between her eyelashes a narrow razor-like blade that cut through in an instant the reddish darkness that had fallen over her mind, thereby slicing through the gloom and leaving in her mind a fissure opening into the future)—even then with the hope (or whatever it's called) that she would awaken and start to see again: to live. Despite the facts. Despite everything.— But she still hadn't told him everything, because she sensed at the moment she was speaking with this man in his white coat, whose name she still didn't know, that even now she was unearthing in herself a glow that could not be and is not called hope, although the source of this feeling lay not in her heart but rather outside of her, pushing into her consciousness and her heart like an unex-pected heat wave: from his voice and in his eyes. And she thought: Hope isn't in my heart, in my hands. *All my hope lies in your words. In the Doctor's eyes.* But maybe she would already have thought: *in your eyes.* For this was an intimate feeling for which one needed no social distance.—But then of course she didn't say it that way; she just shrugged her shoulders:

"I don't know," she said. Then mumbled: ("Maybe just once.")

And then he asked, unexpectedly:

"Do you trust me?" Just like that: "Do you trust me? Or maybe that isn't the right word . . . Anyway, it's all we've got: *trust.*"

"Yes," she said. "I do." If he had asked her that question in a slightly different way or if he had posed it earlier, before time had provided the answer, she would have merely shrugged her shoulders in resignation or she would have lied: "I think I do."

But this was a day or two after she first met him. Or perhaps it had been five or six days since that first meeting. She no longer knew exactly. She remembered their first encounter: it was on the day following her arrival in the camp. They stood side by side in rows, naked, hair shorn; they were mostly young girls, still capable of working or of providing amusement to the German officers leaving for the Eastern Front or returning from there covered in medals and scars: *Deutschland, Deutschland über alles*; they worked doing the selections for the holiday camps: *Deutschland, Deutschland über alles*; only the healthy ones received consideration, pretty young girls who knew how to laugh and who were worthy of Aryan passion and the sperm of an *Übermensch*: *Deutschland, Deutschland über alles!* And that voice sliced like a knife through her exhaustion and her dream-state, speaking at who knows what volume and at an unknown distance from her, just strong enough for her to pick it up, like a whisper, just enough for it tear painfully into her consciousness, to cause her to raise her eyelids; but her own name sounded to her as distant and as alien as if it were coming from some other world. She stared with a vacant, absent look at the white stain of the coat and then her eyes suddenly grew clear as she simultaneously felt and understood that she'd been slapped; then the white stain moved from her iris and a face was projected before her: brown, smoothly brushed hair and two large buckteeth. The woman with the protruding teeth shouted again and drew so near to Marija that she could feel the next slap about to come, but then she heard, from somewhere off to the side:

"Stop! *Damit genug!* We have to be cautious": the voice rose to a falsetto. "I think . . . *Verstehen Sie? . . . Verstehen Sie?*"

"*Ja, ja, ich verstehe . . . Aber ich denke es ist doch nicht. Zu klein. Das Becken wie eines Kindes . . . Aber, insofern, Herr Kollege, denkt sie ist anziehend genüglich . . .*"

"*Du, Abschaum!*" said the man with the yellow star. "Common trash . . . Permit me, Dr. Berta . . ." Behind her, he humbly moved his stethoscope to a spot under her shoulder blades. She was unable to see his face. She only heard his voice. It was the woman with buckteeth, the one they called Dr. Berta, who was asking the questions for her chart. Marija answered with that automatic strength that kicks into action during an onslaught of fear of death or tiredness.

"*Mutan gemišt*—mongrel," said the voice behind her as she rattled off her answers mechanically, thereby laying bare her origins and conjuring up stray ghosts. "Definitely a mongrel."

Then the voice that broke into a falsetto asked: "Would *Frau Judengemischte*—that's what you said your name was, if I'm not mistaken—would *Frau Judengemischte* answer one more question for us? Let's make this . . . essentially off the record, okay?"

Her eyes fixed, as if seeking refuge, on the woman with the protruding teeth, and then they scrolled over the shiny skull of Dr. Nietzsche, finally coming helplessly to rest on the grubby, shadowy square of the nearby window. She clenched her teeth in a desperate effort to transfer her thoughts through the window, outside to that invisible wire bisecting the horizon, but she lacked the power to carry this out. She could hardly think anything at all.

"Don't just stand there. Answer." Then loudly, cynically: "*FRAU JUDENGEMISCHTE! HA HA HA. JUDENGEMISCHTE!*"—and the first part of the sentence was spoken in Polish, whispered, intimate.

Doctor Nietzsche was very taken with her. He grinned.

"*Frau Judengmischte*! Have you ever had occasion to mix some Aryan substance into your mongrel self? I don't mean in terms of your genealogy. Directly. A little pure Aryan fluid. Or any other kind, for that matter?"

The stethoscope on her heart transmitted to Jakob's ear nothing but the waves flooding across the deck and the incantatory beginning of that ancient prayer recognized all over the world both on the sea and dry land: SOS! SOS! SOS! SOS! SOS! SOS!

"No," she said, speaking in time with the slide of the stethoscope in Jakob's hands from left to right, left to right, across her ribs: "No."

"With your permission," Jakob said at that point, laying aside the stethoscope, "in my opinion the *Frau* here is not suitable for such uses. Ordinary trash. A waste of time. Go away! Be gone!"

That had been her first meeting with Jakob, immediately after her arrival in the camp. And that's the reason she was able to answer him a few days later: "*Yes, I do*," when he asked her if she trusted him. That's why she was able, without embarrassment, to bring out the words: "Yes, I do. I believe I do."

Quietly she came to the door and signaled that she was ready. Then he turned off the already dimmed light of the lamp with the shade.

"Žana," she said now in a whisper. "Did I ever tell you: switching on the lamp with the shade was actually a signal for Maks. That's why Jakob had put a lightbulb in it that evening."

"No," said Žana absently. "You never told me about that . . . But sleep now. It's still early. I'd say it's just past midnight. If I haven't completely lost my sense of time." Marija could hear the rustling of the straw beneath Žana and she realized, without opening her eyes, piercing the gloom with them, that Žana was still lying on her stomach in the straw, propped up on her elbows, her eyes fixed on the crack. This position of alertness and the tension in her muscles, like in a cat ready to pounce—this Marija could only interpret as the result of the experience that Žana had gained in the resistance movement, which was hinting something to her again now. Although she had great respect for this sense of caution, so unknown and so nearly masculine to her, a respect likewise inspired by Žana's reflexes, and although she now felt a bit uneasy because of her own passivity, she also considered at least telling Žana about what had happened afterward, but all she said was: "Once I almost saw him. Maks, that is"; Žana repeated her statement from before: "*Devilishly clever fellow. That Maks.*"—Therefore Marija couldn't tell her—anyway not in just a few words—what it was like. That same evening, after the surprise visit from Dr. Nietzsche. Less than an hour afterward. As soon as she had left Jakob's room.

After he had turned off the lamp with the shade, Jakob listened intently and then carefully unlocked the door. The only other thing she remembered was an embrace in the dark and the pressure of his body. Then she slid along the wall down the darkened corridor in the barracks. She could almost recall how many steps she took, feeling the grim cold wall all the while. Then it happened, not even twenty minutes after Dr. Nietzsche's departure. That's when the invisible but omnipresent Maks appeared again, out of the darkness. And this is how it went: no sooner had she taken ten steps (with one hand extended into the void before her like a sleepwalker and the other resting against the wall) she felt a sharp pain in her shin and realized in that moment that she had knocked over something that would now echo through the whole barrack and that would be heard from one end of the hall to the other. At the same time she heard, from the end of the corridor, HALT! HALT! and the clacking steps of iron-shod boots. All she knew, all she could know at that moment, was that there was no way back into Jakob's room, for it was already too late for that. She merely clung to the wall (what would have Žana done at a time like this?) and groped her way to a door. No option remained to her (the door was locked) other than to wait here for the brightening of the sharp beam from the flashlight sweeping murderously through the corridor right in front of her nose. From her precarious haven she could see one end of the heavy wooden bench that she had overturned with her leg and that was now lying lethargically on its back, like some sort of felled animal squirming in agony: the shadow of its fettered legs twisted and flickered in the backlighting of the oblique, whirling beam of the flashlight. She sensed that in a few moments the lethal ray would blind her and she would contort and carbonize as if struck by lightning, but before this thought could sink in completely and she could carbonize and turn black totally by herself as she shuddered with

horror, she felt a giant hand grabbing her from somewhere behind her back, covering her mouth, and that same hand, in the
same motion with which it had already yanked away the support
behind her back, or so it seemed to her, pulled on her so that for
a moment she was suspended in the air as if falling into a swim-
ming pool or like when someone pulls a chair out from under
you in that moment when you drop onto it tired and anticipating but find an emptiness much deeper than the chair itself, and
then that hand pulled her somewhere up and back without unglu-
ing itself from her mouth. Thus, barely comprehending what was
happening to her, as if she had just woken up, she could hear the
banging on the door and she realized simultaneously (as if that
same knocking had revived her) that she was now in a safer refuge
than she had been in a few moments ago when she was standing
there glued to the wall: crammed under the bed where the invisible hand of the *deus ex machina* had stowed her in haste, she
could only hear how the *deus ex machina* moved away from her
hiding place with powerful slaps of his clogs and how he unlocked
the door, and then she could see the beam of the flashlight, which
wavered like the flame of a candle, slice through the narrow crack
between the floor and the rough blanket hanging over the edge of
the bed under which she was ensconced.

"What's going on?" said the man in the clogs.

"Patrol!" came the voice of the bloodhound: "Somebody's mess-
ing around in the hallway."

"I did hear something crashing about," said *deus ex machina*.
"As if someone were overturning that bench. I'd just gotten back
from headquarters. (I worked the night shift.) And I had just fallen

asleep, when something went bang. And I remembered that somebody had put a bench out there yesterday."

"Who could have knocked it over? Exiting the premises is forbidden now. It just struck three A.M."

And Maks said:

"It had to be one of those women from the other end of the barracks."

The steps of the bloodhound receded and Marija could hear Maks closing the door.

"Stay here until the barking quiets down": in the darkness she couldn't see his face. "Are you injured?"

"No," she said. "I scraped my shin a bit . . . Trivial detail, compared to what could have happened." Then she added: "Just a trifle . . . Maks."

That's why she told Žana: "I almost saw him one time. Maks, that is."

6

And now she thought once more—still lying there motionless and watchful next to her child—among a great burst of other thoughts about the future (in the distance, the artillery had again begun to sing): *How will I find Jakob?* Quite directly, and barely acknowledging the sense of peace and security with which she said this to herself, she thought once again: *How will I find Jakob?* as though that were the only thing remaining to do and as if she were thinking all this from the other side, outside of the wire and outside of the past, even outside of the present: as if this thought had begun to take wing from some already achieved future here at one's fingertips; all that separated her from it was an insignificant revolution of the clock and two or three relaxed steps as when you're heading out on an excursion and the shady woods come into view and you begin to smell the wildflowers and conifers and there's a bit of something to eat in the basket along with a thermos and white napkins and all you have to do is sprawl out on the grass and take out the tablecloth and spread it out over the same rustling green grass: and in her mind reverberated, almost audibly, the words HOW WILL I FIND JAKOB? like a *leitmotif* that disappears and then rushes back in more and more powerful bursts. She had wanted to say to Žana *How will I find Jakob* so that Žana would notice that she wasn't sleeping but then it occurred to her that if she were to announce her thought aloud then it might flinch at the immediate future and collide with this grubby barracks, with Polja's dead body, and with all the rest of it, and then it would plummet into the straw and remain lying there like a bloody bird with a bullet wound that trembles and squirms before it croaks; and this wouldn't only happen if she were to say it aloud like that, *How will I find Jakob*, but really even the fact that she would think it, thereby clearly underscoring that there was no longer any doubt in her mind about Jakob's freedom or her own—even that was enough to set off a revival of doubt. That decisively articulated thought, aimed squarely at the future, was enough to turn all of her thoughts around toward the past, like a triple echo. Anyway it was only because her newborn thought was incapable of locating Jakob in a clear future perspective that she devoted herself with all her strength to a Jakob who was nonetheless more reliable in the past. And in the present, of course. Therefore she said nothing to Žana. Even if she wanted to say it the way it had arisen in her consciousness—it would be too late. Her thoughts were already seeking a different Jakob in the past. A less optimistic Jakob. But clearer, more real. He was still the only genuine Jakob, perhaps no longer of flesh and blood but only a frozen film frame in her mind: he stands there with raised hands, making some restrained gesture (the way she had last seen him): momentum at a standstill.

That was the most recent and only real Jakob, the last one she'd seen with her own eyes. Not, therefore, the phantomlike and unreal Jakob about whom she was receiving news through the even less visible Maks. For how could she have a clear conception of Jakob when from somewhere or other, like a bolt from the blue or straight out of hell itself, she'd get coded messages like "The trip went fine" or "The weather was nice" and all sorts of other such meteorological issues in which she was supposed to, first of all, unearth a meaning such as "Jakob has been moved" or "Jakob will contact you" and so forth, but also, secondly, discover under all of it a living, real character, that of Jakob. Even the infrequent oral statements that reached her third-hand from Jakob by way of Maks's representatives, even these reports didn't help her much to *see* Jakob—nothing did—apart, of course, from things she remembered, insofar as she had any memory at all and could recognize even for a moment the face that with all of her powers she was always trying to call to mind.

She remembered: at that time all of the women who had arrived with her were already dead, likewise all those who had replaced them in her barracks in Auschwitz. She no longer recalled faces, more just columns of skeletal reminiscences. Though faceless, she could still however remember some, maybe even all of the women she had gotten to know during those days when a mechanical hand wasn't dispatching each and every one of those countenances into oblivion; though mainly recalled the Babylonian confusion of languages, the times when somebody, so-and-so, would slip through the fingers of that mechanical hand, especially when it was one of the early arrivals, one of those that formed a solemn procession ending with Polja, who was now lying there dead beside her. The first was Eržika Ignac. The one who Dr. Nietzsche picked right at the beginning, as a guinea pig. Then Nameless, who played in the prisoners' orchestra;—but the mechanical hand that would light a red light to warn of rebellion and go into action to sever contact before any misfortune could occur, or at least before the great shock of a dose of high-voltage current arrived, that hand had now compressed the column of women with one powerful sweep and covered it up with a clean white shroud of the type placed on the catafalques of heroes or virgins; Marija was the only one, the only one for a long time now, who stood next to that catafalque like a soldier who by some miracle had remained alive after the explosion of a bomb that fell into the trench where his unit was fighting, and who now stands bare-headed next to the mass grave, with flowers in hand, reading from the marble the names of those who had been his comrades-in-arms and with whom he had shared his cigarettes and exchanged in moments of weakness family photographs and memories, and who now in anguish thinks back to all of those friends at rest under the marble obelisk, transformed into golden letters, and he wonders how this could be, by dint of what miracle had he missed being part of the formation at that final roll call, for his place was there, in that line, right alongside the first in the row, who was A, and the one behind, who was C, and whose names were now impressed in the marble of the monument.

That's how she felt now in front of the obelisk of memories: standing with a bouquet of flowers and amazed, hardly believing her eyes. Consequently she now needed to search for Jakob in her memory, there where she had left him nearly an eternity ago, actually not quite a year ago, if one assumes that at some point she really took leave of him, for in all honesty spiritual presence is itself nothing more than a marble obelisk, but now she wanted to find *that* Jakob, the one who was more than an obelisk perpetually present, because an obelisk is raised to those who are absent for good, which is the same thing as death, albeit a somewhat nicer way of saying it.

She had received a message from Jakob to the effect that the camp was going to be evacuated (so it could be host to a new wave) and that Maks had bribed the guards with jewelry that he had discovered in a secret hiding place. Then, with the combined help of Jakob and Maks, she was transferred to Birkenau, thus skirting death once more, although she had to part from Jakob. Maybe forever. But she still knew, when they separated her from him, that she would have to see him again, even if it was only once more; she felt, undeniably, that she *would have to see Jakob*. Especially when she grasped that she was not only his wife but also the mother of his child. She thought back to that meeting: she recognized him then, the first time since their parting, right at the moment he stood up and then bent down again to lift something that lay next to the coffin by his boot-clad feet. But just now she wasn't even certain that it was he, although this man in his white hospital coat (he was standing sideways in front of her, leaning against the enormous wooden crate that reached the level of his chest, while with his right hand he was brandishing a hammer, and she, a short distance away, would see his arm first rising and then, not simultaneously but just an instant later, hear the dull impact, as though she were watching from a great distance as someone split wood) bore many similarities to Jakob, and she could recognize him also by the jolt with which her body had made this known even before in her consciousness that lightbulb with the label JAKOB blared it out as well; for the first few months, since she arrived at Birkenau, since the last time she had seen Jakob before her transfer, everything that had happened to her seemed unreal, as if the world now needed thorough verification through a prodigious effort of her senses and her brain, for slowly everything seemed to be turning into a dream or delirium that would resist casual authentication by the senses;—but then she'd caught sight of his profile, his brow, and the soldiers who were standing beside him and next to the enormous wooden crate with widely spread legs helped her dispel these doubts, not because soldiers with machine guns couldn't belong to a dream legion (having infiltrated her dreams from the real world) but because she was already used to dreams about Jakob staged in a well-nigh absurd setting, strange even for a dream: intimate, gentle light filling a room, with the almost unreal radiance of an aureole; or: a landscape illuminated by sunlight, softness like the backdrop of a photograph in which he, Jakob, appears; nevertheless she started to read once more, after innumerable times, the sign above the camp entrance surrounded by barbed wire: ARBEIT UND FREIHEIT and then TIEHIERF DNU TIEBRA, as if the very fact of her reading the sign backward authenticated this reality in the midst of which she had glimpsed Jakob standing there in his white hospital coat, tall, with his swinging hammer, so similar to himself and so unreal, both apotheosis and phantom. She figured out when her column would draw even with him and she strained, with all her might, to devise for that brief instant the cleverest and most earnest manner of exploiting this miraculous meeting (they were moving along four to a row, heads shorn, covered in mud, in greasy convicts' clothing with dingy yellow stars, dragging their bloodied and blistered feet in heavy, tattered clogs through the sodden sleet, spades on their shoulders and singing "The Girl I Adore," a song that they'd learned from the prisoners at the work site and that they always sang as they returned to camp)—and to call out to him that she too was there among those singing scarecrows and that she couldn't hold out any longer; feverishly she wondered how she would shout to him, with what words and in what tone of voice, that she was there and that she was pregnant and that she was incapable of doing anything save yelling JAKOB, I AM PREGNANT, which would be the end of it all; and before she had succeeded in choosing the shortest and most resonant word (as with a poet who in a flight of inspiration has nothing to choose because the one and only correct word is coming, pouring, out of him, as if by its own accord), and before she grasped or in the very instant she grasped that in two or three minutes it would be too late for anything because the cohort was turning left, JAKOB, I AM PREGNANT flashed through her mind and simultaneously she heard her own voice breaking into the open air and boring like a bullet through the flapping cloak of the song "The Girl I Adore" and immediately thereafter she felt, before the satisfaction of having done it, or rather of doing everything she could so that Jakob would hear her, before that she felt the fear of punishment: when she felt the dull blow in her ribs she had already been obsessed with this thought and the fear (as if this thought had shattered against her head with more force than the rubber club in her ribs) that none of this had anything to do with Jakob and that he had not been transformed in the Germans' eyes but only in hers and that he really didn't care whether she kept the child for how was it possible that he hadn't stopped brandishing the hammer in his hand (she cried out during that infinitely small portion of a second when the hammer in his hand had reached its point of maximum height and stopped moving, in order to change direction, as if she had been waiting precisely for that sign and as if she were afraid that the next swing of his arm would slice through her decision, her voice), how was it possible that he didn't turn his head or a muscle didn't twitch on his face or that he didn't at the very least give her a wink.—Jakob in his white hospital coat with the Moses-like motion of his right hand: that image remained engraved in her consciousness like a picture of the crucified Christ that she had seen once, long ago, when she was still a child, in a film being shown—in a village in the Vojvodina where along with her mother she was spending a few weeks of vacation—by Catholic missionaries in a village school, not too long prior to the war: hair waving in the wind above the high, anguished brow of the young crucified Christ (that was her very first movie, since her father had still never allowed her to go to the cinema)—and then through the hall ran the sound of prayers and petitions and the weeping of pious ladies as if they were witnessing a holy instance of unexpected epiphany and then the young friar stopped the wind and the hair ceased its fluttering above Christ's pale countenance, though his eyes were still looking out with vanquished meekness and the people fell to their knees, sobbing:—in this way Jakob's figure in its white hospital coat and with its upraised arm engraved itself on her consciousness, crucified between two robbers. And while her unit, right after that, in the dead, ominous quiet listened to the announcements and roll call on the hellish, muddy grounds of the camp (the dead they carried from the worksite on their backs and placed in formation at their old spots, straightening their shorn, mud-covered skulls with the point of their bulky clogs), they too stopped her movie but that petrified swing of his arm with its hammer still preyed more upon her mind than the fear of punishment; just when she heard her number, her name, when that five-digit stamp slapped her in the face and began to sizzle and pop in her flesh and heart, it seemed to her that the interrupted arc started to move once more and then that the raised arm with its hammer had suddenly descended onto her head (the young friar started up the film projector again: the arrested moment soared back into motion, the hair fluttered again above the pale, martyred countenance of the young Christ); but then, as she went between the two rows of cudgellers down the narrow corridor to her cell (she hadn't seen their faces, only felt the swings of the arms with bastinados that came down everywhere on her body: blunt and knotted pains on her ribs and stomach and head) she was still watching in her nearly extinguished consciousness nothing but the multiplied image of a man wielding a hammer and bringing it down on her head. (And then the movie was over and darkness came upon the little village school and the women wiped their tear-stained eyes and kissed the hands and feet of the young missionary like those of a medium on an intimate footing with the supreme being and someone rang the bell in the village church and the leaden, pious sound of its copper quivered in the air like intense heat, and Ilonka Kutaj said to her, back then, coming home from school: "Your father crucified Christ": and then she added, so that people could see what she meant when she said "Your father crucified Christ":—"Or he at least gave them the nails," and then she continued: "And you gave them nails, too," and Ilonka's mother told her: "Stop talking that way, sweetheart, as though Marija were guilty. She wasn't even born yet, and neither was her father," but then Ilonka jeered: "Neither was her great-great-grandfather," and then: "You told me yourself that all the Jews are responsible for the death of the Son of God;—that's what you said—they contributed the nails at least; and didn't I hear you say that at least five hundred and fifty million times, a billion times, a trillion?"

7

In this way Marija slipped into unconsciousness (even before she reached her dormitory at the end of the corridor), under the cruel sign of those hands in motion and the frozen film; the last thing she heard was the bitter reproach directed at her by Ilonka Kutaj way back when, in the village school one day after Epiphany: "If nothing else they brought the nails."

She recalled that summer in the village, and her own marveling eyes, the eyes of a city girl, although she was over ten years old at the time; she could also still remember the voice in which her father had spoken to her when she had come back home early, had left the village, so that his words would forever (and even now) remain in her mind, and the meadow under a blanket of flowers and the outing to the forest, but before that: the cornflower blooming in the mature rye and the sun high above their heads, and then the beckoning of the forest and the clearing and the promised shade and all the rest of it: the white linen on the green dining table and the thermos with its thick, cool milk—and then once more her mother's voice (she's sitting next to her in the grass, hugging her knees to herself and resting her beautiful head on them and Marija can still see the neat knot in her hair done up in a bun):

"What are we going to tell Father?" but first she let Marija (naturally) drink the milk from the thermos and eat the leg of goose and the poppy-seed pastry and only then did she ask: "What will you say to Father?" but Marija still couldn't understand what was so important about all of this that it would make her mother cross and her mother sat there absorbed in thought and didn't end up with even a crumb of anything at all to eat, not even a wee cup of milk, and why is it that one can't simply say to Father: "I ran away from Ilonka Kutaj, who had offended me and who I will not talk to anymore and who I don't ever want to see again," and then, if Father should ask how Ilonka Kutaj had offended her, she would tell him in a simple and precise manner: and then he might well not be annoyed and not send her back to the village, but if he were to try to convince her to do so, she would say to him: *she also insulted you; you and your great-great-great-grandfather*; and back there in the forest before Mother had gathered up all the white napkins and strewn the crumbs on top of a tree stump for the birds and the ants, and even before she had said to her out of worry and fright:

"You may not tell your father that; we cannot tell him the real reason," she was already firmly convinced that in the end she would have to tell him everything, even the part about the distant ancestor, and she enjoyed imagining him, that is to say her father, putting his rifle down in front of her, an insignificant little girl, and how he would stand there disarmed and dumbfounded with the short little pipe that he had just removed from his mouth, and she saw her words wash away that penetrating, severe look behind the steel-framed spectacles; exactly as it was, exactly the way she knew it would be; but she had already decided back then, in the forest, that she would only tell it if worse came to worse, even if she had promised her mother that she wouldn't say anything under any circumstances, other than (naturally) what Mother would say, that is, that she didn't like it in the village and that she had come down with diarrhea and had caught measles.

She remembered the return from the village, and her perplexity at not traveling by train (the way they had come) and only then by cart through the fields of rye and poppies, but they covered the whole distance back in a cart, moving continuously alongside the tracks with their thundering, haughty trains, and she loved traveling by train, as did her mother, who had told her that she loved to travel by train, but just now she said she preferred to lurch along the bumpy village lanes, where there isn't any way to shield your head and so the sun strikes you directly on the pate, right on the crown of your skull. Then they reached the city and Marija said to her mother that she'd had more than enough of this cart and that she would at least like to ride the streetcar at this point, to ride the blue one that went from the train station straight to the corner of their street where the chestnut blossoms were, and she saw, the moment their cart turned past the station: first the tram's lyre-shaped pantograph, and then the fiacres and the horses snorting in front of the station: and then that little blue streetcar appeared, with a tinkling noise like that of small bells, the streetcar that looked so much like a toy, and she cried out:

"There's the blue one!"—as if she had run into a neighbor from her building or a classmate or at least run across one of her toys, because she enjoyed riding on this blue streetcar and the blue ones are less common and are prettier, because it's not at all a matter of indifference whether they are blue or yellow, it matters a great deal, but instead of stopping at the station and knocking the dust off their clothes and finally sending away the cart with the worn-out horses, her mother pointed out the way to the driver in his thick sheep's-wool coat (she who had been wondering the whole time how he could stand to wear it in this intolerable heat), and Marija said to her mother in a pitiful, imploring voice *Aren't we taking the streetcar?* and it seemed, in the midst of so much consternation, that it was simply a matter perhaps of inviting her mother to remember by means of this exclamation the thing that she had perhaps forgotten in the village, namely that you could ride the streetcar all the way to their house, perhaps she had merely overlooked the comfort and other advantages of the streetcar as compared to an ordinary team of horses. And Marija thought that as soon as her mother heard her question and as soon as she had been brought to her senses she would clap her hand to her forehead and laugh about her forgetfulness and say something like, "Aha, you see, I had totally forgotten the streetcar," but her mother didn't clap her hand to her forehead and she didn't say it, for the first little while she didn't say anything, in fact, but just sat there and looked straight ahead, acting as though she couldn't hear her daughter and as though looking at the façades of the houses so delighted her that she actually couldn't hear anything at the moment, nothing at all. Therefore Marija had to express her amazement again, but now (for the sake of caution) with a bit of humor in her voice, as if she were saying, "Hey, want to guess what we forgot?" and as if she had to laugh in anticipation of the way her mother would clap her hand to her forehead and reply, for instance, "The thermos!" and Marija would then produce it from her little travel bag and laugh at herself, naturally, laugh; but none of that occurred, and instead of marveling and laughing, her mother, barely turning her head, said:

Riding the streetcar is forbidden, and before Marija could feel astonishment at that, her mother continued: "That's the reason you aren't allowed to tell your father why you got mad at Ilonka Kutaj." And that was the first time Marija put various facts together and finally comprehended more or less why they had kept her in the village with the excuse that it was good for her health, and why she couldn't tell the father anything, but precisely because it was still not entirely clear to her and something was still concealed from her she resolved firmly to tell her father everything, naturally not right away, but she would definitely find a good reason to force herself to say it, and she would come up with an excuse to use on her mother and on herself, thus she said to her mother now, as if she couldn't even understand the little bit that she did understand or suspect:

"I don't understand why it's forbidden to ride the streetcar! I just don't understand . . . how could riding a streetcar can be forbidden?"—And at that point mother tapped her head, not in the way she would if something had crossed her mind, or not just in that way, Marija saw her mother raising her hand to her forehead and holding it there, not as someone would if they were wondering about something but as if she were brushing away a broken-hearted resolution from her forehead along with a strand of hair, and then Marija continued watching as her mother stretched her arm out with the same hopeless gesture in the direction where the streetcar stood, like a toy, and her mother stared, still searching with her eyes *I don't understand why riding the streetcar is forbidden* as if she were seeing a streetcar for the first time, wondering, lips pursed, what purpose that blue tin can with the lyre on top served, whether it was a vehicle or a children's toy or maybe something even more obscure, maybe a dangerous or even a sinful thing; and then Marija heard her mother' voice, like a rebuke:

"My God, you aren't a child anymore! Haven't you seen anything around you that might give you a hint?" and then, as if she were pointing out the letters in a primer to someone just learning their alphabet or pretending not to know what was what or even that he couldn't see them: "Read that. There, you see, the white letters. By the door . . . Do you understand? You speak good German . . . Yes, that placard on the streetcar. Next to the door. FÜR JUDEN VERBOTEN. Do you understand: *für Juden verboten?* Do you understand now?"—and Marija grasped it all immediately, at least as far as the translation from German went, of all things her mother hadn't needed to translate that, but she understood something else too in the murky fabric of events, though still she felt she hadn't been given sufficient cause to alter the expression on her face or to stop pursing her own lips like that, like a cantankerous little witch, and then she resolved firmly and just out of spite to tell her father everything anyway, in order to find out the remainder of what she didn't know, the remainder of the truth that was still hiding from her but that she must ultimately find out, lest she remain or become a genuinely cantankerous witch and go on pursing her lips forever, or at least until she finally came to know what it meant that people all of a sudden, while she'd been in the village, had written FÜR JUDEN VERBOTEN on the streetcars, which is to say *why* this was so, why she was no longer allowed to ride on the streetcar,

> *What about the yellow one, Mama*
> *Not the yellow one either*
> child, you aren't allowed on any streetcar
> understand: *not any*
> *But can Ilonka Kutaj ride them?*

Yes, Ilonka Kutaj for instance, that chatterbox stupid louse-ridden ignoramus urchin D-student at the bottom of the class on whose account Marija had to flee her village and get into an argument with her mother and now she'll have to have one with her father too and she'll quarrel with the entire world if necessary, she'll put on a pouty face even if it makes her uglier than the ugliest tooth-less crone, Ilonka Kutaj had made her that mad; and even now she could still hear the voice of her father (he had started speaking all at once after everything she had dumped on him so she knew she had done the right thing in telling him everything even if she had no real reason to because her father hadn't been irritated when her mother said that they had returned because they weren't enjoying the village and because Marija had gotten diarrhea and the mea-sles because she was allergic to the village diet, he'd only said "It would have been better if you had stayed there and stuck it out, until *things here* calm down"), she knew that she had done the smart thing in telling her father everything regardless, everything, even the part about the insult and the great-great-grandfather and he—that is, her father—was not only disarmed but even more so cut off at the knees, he had become a pitiful creature, so that Marija had even begun sympathizing with him and regretting not listening to her mother and keeping quiet about everything; in a gesture of despair he simply took the short pipe out of his mouth and she saw the way his austere gaze grew blurry and faded under his spectacles in their steel frame and then focused onto a painful, desperate decision (precisely, by the way, in the way she had foreseen this happening) until a speech burst out of him all at once flowing like water so that even now she was still wondering why he had spoken with so much intensity which had ensured that despite everything she remembered all of it, and which also meant that she must really have understood it all long beforehand:—"*It is not the hatred of Negroes of Irish or of Jews that is at issue here, and it's thus not an ethnic or racial or national collective or group that is at issue but rather it is simply human intolerance that is searching for a pretext in skin color or in customs or in anything else that is different from what is generally found in a given setting; it is the inherent and deeply rooted human passion (if not nature, which would perhaps be more exact and which is perhaps the most accurate means of description but I will not concede that to anyone not even to myself and least of all to you), the passion, that is, for mistreating and humiliating the person who otherwise is happily referred to as your neighbor; or else (most precisely of all perhaps): it is the atavism of the horde and of the animal that seeks to overpower and annihilate all other species and all other creatures and to establish dominion and that triumphs for the most ordinary and egotisti-*

cal reasons (but not the reason you probably thought of right away I mean the so-called survival of the fittest) (that they also teach in schools supported by examples from biology and zoology) and to which one can give no other name than refined atavism, and it is something completely different and more beastly than any natural selection that is incidentally to be found to the same degree in humans as among animals; because if the struggle for the survival of our species were the only thing at stake here then injustice crime and violence would not be tolerated or would at least not be tolerated in the name of specific racist national principles and prejudices and people wouldn't say A Negro or A Jewish child was killed but instead would say only A CHILD WAS KILLED and idiotic questions would not be posed about skin color or religion which help people reduce culpability or shed it altogether; by such questions you arrive at an answer that is in essence absurd because it isn't actually an answer: I mean that one is using such a question put in that way to arrive at the excuse of *otherness* (naturally with reference to your larger ethnic or national or religious whole) and from this it follows that no one under God's blue sky can be blamed for anything but rather what is to blame is this totally idiotic thing that one can call *otherness,* which allows the responsibility to be lifted not only from the individual but from humans altogether since the culprit is an abstract guilty party and their guilt consequently an abstract guilt; *needless to say nothing is easier than inventing a reason for hatred and thus also a justification for crime: one needs merely to ascribe to a less numerous therefore weaker ethnic or religious or national group one of the common human vices or one of the universal human failings (not even a sin) such as for example greed stinginess stupidity or a proclivity to drink or whatever else might be in this case made out to be after all a mortal sin: in this manner you accomplish several of the things that are required in order to commit a crime that is a priori justified: the victim is stigmatized (for he or she has been grouped under the sign of uniformity of skin color or faith and one of those vices that is common to all) (and this vice is most often selected arbitrarily and according to some obvious characteristic that is then interpreted as an indication of the very opposite essence) thereby covering up that same universal vice in the person doing the stigmatizing, and then the finger is forever pointed at him that is to say at the stigmatized one who has been proclaimed the incarnation of one or several shared vices and through this, that is by means of this sophisticated atavism, the human being that I have already mentioned has free reign to act out unfettered his destructive and sadistic bestial passions on those who bear the communal stigma of one particular skin race faith or set of customs"*—and he nervously knocked his pipe against the edge of the table, scattering its ashes and glowing bits on the carpet, as if he regretted revealing all this in so chaotic a fashion and with such horrible and grim vagueness to a fourteen-year old girl who could not understand, couldn't grasp any of it, but the situation had become clear to her right at the beginning (or so she thought), for after the first two or three sentences he was no longer really addressing himself to her but rather (more or less) to her mother, who most likely was just looking at him with alarm and nodding in agreement, as if she wanted to make sure he understood her agreement, as though saying "Yes, yes, absolutely," yet Marija knew that everything he was saying would eventually enrage her father (and her mother must have known this too, because Marija's father didn't like to talk too much and had only begun doing so since he started drinking, and this very recently, since everything had gone wrong and he had lost his job; heaven knows they weren't rich but her father had invested everything in some business and then things had gone south and he had started working as an hourly employee and as the purchasing agent and foreign-language correspondent clerk for a brush manufacturer, and when he had started drinking, people said to her mother, "Odd, really odd. I've never known a Jew who hit the bottle," that's what Mrs. Vajs said anyway; and one evening Aunt Lela said: "You are the one woman hapless enough to find a drinker among the Jews") and that's exactly how it turned out in the end; that evening he really tied one on and he smashed two or three coffee cups, thereby breaking up and spoiling the whole coffee service, and then he called for Marija to come and ordered her to remove his shoes, something he had never done before; she remembered the way his face loomed over her as she undid his laces caked in vomit, and she remembered also the concerned look on her mother's face as she stood right there the entire time but acted as if she was completely preoccupied with grinding the coffee, but she knew that her mother was aching and hesitating and biting her tongue, and she then (nevertheless) said in her barely audible voice, scared to death quaking imploring:

"Edi, please, Edi, leave the child alone. I'll take your shoes off. She's still tired out from the trip. Can't you see that she's tired?" and then, after a brief, perilous interval, her father's voice rang out:

"She ought to get used to it . . . Soon she won't have a choice. All girls . . ." Then once more her mother's outcry:

"Edi! Please, Edi! Don't be cruel to the child." And her father's voice again:

"Our young lady doesn't even know what it means to be forbidden to ride the streetcar . . ."

("Edi, I beg you!")

" . . . or what FÜR JUDEN VERBOTEN means; well now, she should learn it then; it's high time she learns, and *when, if not now*?": and then he said, having miraculously sobered up all at once (at least it appeared that way to her eyes or maybe it was also because he had put his glasses with the steel frames back on, as when he was getting ready to quiz her about her German lessons):—"Come on then, give your nose a good blow with my handkerchief, sweetie"—and he wiped her nose with his handkerchief that stunk of tobacco, as did his fingers, and he went on to say to her that she should go wash her hands and bring him the German dictionary, but there was no way for her to foresee what he was getting at and why it had occurred to him to give her a vocabulary quiz now in the middle of vacation:—but there he was already holding the book pressed to his chest, the same way women do with prayer books or lousy orators do with their cheat sheets (and her mother was still standing to the side, and it seemed either that she didn't know what she should do or that she was simply waiting to see what he, her father that is, would do next), and without opening the dictionary so much as a single time, for neither she nor he had need of that, he asked Marija how to say in German: *to think, to breathe, to live, to love* and several other verbs that have now slipped her mind, and as she was answering without pausing to ponder he merely uttered "Bravo" after every word and nodded like a professor, and then, at the end, after one final "bravo," he said:

"Now the young lady should insert in the appropriate place the words VERBOTEN and FÜR JUDEN VERBOTEN" and her mother could only cry out one more time:

"Edi! For heaven's sake, Edi! I beg you!"

8

Nevertheless it had happened at the best possible time, she thought. At the best possible time: it was a few hours after she had caught sight of Jakob and shouted out to him, Jacob, I AM PREGNANT. She lay in the hay and even before she'd opened her eyes and completely regained consciousness she thought that at any rate it had happened at the best possible time, because as soon as she heard the kittenlike crying of the child she understood everything and she recalled Aunt Lela's voice saying: "Children that are born in the seventh month are only proving that they're curious about life." That's what she'd said to Anijela when she delivered a baby prematurely, but Anijela's little boy died after two or three days and at that point Aunt Lela told her the truth: that the child hadn't been born in the seventh month but in the eighth, because if it had been born in the seventh it might have lived; but at least it hadn't felt any pain, just more of a mortal tiredness, nothing more than a sort of nightmare, as one might have during a heavy sleep. Marija was still partly in shock and at any given time could sink away only then re-emerge once more on the surface. Now— lying alongside deceased Polja and the child—she remembered it all: she wanted to think *Child* and she wanted to think *Jakob's child* (she didn't know if she'd really heard it or if she only seemed to have heard Žana's voice saying A SON! A SON! in her half-sleep in her delirium like an angel announcing to Marija with flowers the birth of the Son of God), but just as that bittersweet thought struck she would become disoriented as if from a strong dose of morphine or some otherworldly fragrance; something clutched at her stomach and she thought that it was just the end of the month approaching and nothing worse would be involved than putting on a pad just in case and she already carried a bit of cotton in her handbag (her period always came unpredictably like this); then she rushed to get ready and said to her mother *I have some kind of pain in my stomach. Maybe it was that pâté. Do you think it's because of the pâté?* but her mother said *No, today is the 22nd and you'll be getting your period soon; it would be better if you didn't go to the theater,* and then Marija got scared that her mother would make her stay home and so she tried to say indifferently *it's nothing serious it was just one little twinge; everything's fine again now; I'll put on a pad just in case,* and her mother said *You can go to the theater any day* but still Marija grabbed her purse and rushed to the streetcar stop and she wished she hadn't forgotten the pads because her stomach clenched again and an old man with a moronic look on his face and big bags under his eyes and a stiff, starched collar pressed against her stomach with his elbow but she couldn't switch seats because of the crowd in the theater in which she was now perishing for lack of oxygen. But as the curtain rose and the performance began (in her haste she hadn't managed to see what was playing and now she was ashamed to ask anyone) the thing in her stomach began to grow more and more painful; *I might not be able to follow the plot because of these stomach pains*, she thought, it's a pantomime of some sort, it would be good just to ask somebody, and she turned to the left to get someone's elbow off of her stomach and she saw that it was the same old man with the stiff collar and the expansive circles under his eyes: "Please move your elbow," she said, but the old man must have been deaf or was pretending to be deaf because he didn't so much as bat an eye though someone behind them whispered "ssssh" and she had to squeeze over to one side of her seat and twist her back in such a way that she felt like she was tied into a knot; *Rotten old man* she thought even while deciding to try nonetheless to follow the play although she understood nothing and actually it was in a foreign language out of which a few familiar words rang, which made it seem to her for a moment that it could be *Faust* or some Biblical legend or something like that for all at once light flashed on the stage and she saw a man in polished boots and a uniform, with a whip in his hand and she was horror-struck to recognize him as *Obersturmbannführer* Hirsch and she understood how strange it was that he should materialize in this performance and she abruptly grasped in her chaotic dread the absurdity of these temporal and spatial phenomena, which rapidly became almost self-explanatory to her, but she was in no condition to think and to exclaim I AM DREAMING THIS I AM DREAMING THIS instead she just continued sitting and all she could feel was her belly knotting up with terror and it's like her legs were paralyzed or tied to the chair by the eyes of the phantom-like *Obersturmbannführer* Hirsch and she remembered that she hadn't brought along her sanitary napkins and she felt the sticky fluid slipping down her thighs but she rallied enough strength to rise from her seat with a loud and painful bang and at once she felt her insides breaking open and she felt herself falling, prone, into a dazzling vertiginous abyss. The other thing she remembered then, a little later, was Žana's voice: "Polja, we have to wash her," and then: "That eased her pain," and then right after that the opaque realization arrived that she had given birth even before she grasped the fact that Polja was washing her dress and she sensed with tormented bliss that Žana had placed the child next to her and she heard the kittenlike crying of a baby and Žana's whisper like Mary's annunciation: "*Premier-né d'Israël!*" and all at once she recalled everything: tracing her thoughts backward across a blurry trail until she reached a still darker past: she recalled the dream and Jakob and Aunt Lela's voice and her father's bitter alcohol-tinged words that night when she returned from the village; and now (still lying on her back, frozen through but excited to have the child on her chest, feeling his warmth permeate her as if at this moment their blood and their flesh were mingling, feeling the baby that awakened and drank deeply from her breast and emptied himself into her and mixed his blood with hers, as if in that moment, here on the border of a new epoch very nearly physically present, a time in her and therefore also in her child's history, all the currents of blood were merging) she felt faced with this magnificent something that she was supposed to encounter and the presence of which she sensed in and around herself, the same vague sensation of the moment being not only familial but also historical, the same feeling that her father must have had on the night before the raid. Because it looked as though death, or birth, was supposed to intervene (from the familial and historical points of view, they were the same thing) in the daily course of events, as if a person could imagine himself or herself above a river of that blood out of which we surface and into which we once more sink and which flows, invisible as an underground river, within us, and that we catch sight of precisely at those moments when obscure new currents are created within its flow or when floods break out or when a drought comes and the river starts to recede. Her father must not have been aware himself of what actually turned his thoughts in that direction and what impelled him on that evening immediately before they were to take him away to start making his last speech, to begin speaking with her or at least in her vicinity (she had just turned fourteen) in the same way as he could usually converse only with the elder Mr. Rozenberg—maybe. Now she realized that her father had said what he said—ten days after that night he'd been drunk and she had taken off his slimy shoes—at a moment precisely akin to this current one, that is to say like this very span of a few hours tonight separating her from escape or death and that possessed a density greater than an ordinary night by at least the degree to which the air here in the barracks was denser than the night air outside, hours that weren't noted in red oil paint on the calendar of blood for the family or history but the density of which is filled with new perceptions and presentiments: it must be that those hours about which her father had spoken to her possessed a specific heaviness, for he had told her that "the *ancient rising of the blood* can be felt then, rising from its veiled wellspring in the guts of our most distant progenitors and reaching all the way to some descendant in the distant future; I mean, it's possible," he said on that evening, not knowing himself that it was his valedictory talk with life, with the message carried in his blood, if one may put it that way, but without doubt it must have been that he wasn't too far away from an almost metaphysical presentiment, "as in some ancient religions, a belief not in the transparent illusion of life beyond the grave, like we have in the Jewish or Christian faiths, but believing in the indestructibility of that part of the human being representing an indispensable and necessary link in the chain created by nature; and in which case it isn't of vital interest (vital of course for nature though not for us, and maybe not even for us if we were able to look at everything through different eyes, from a standpoint broader than that of a human being—that's what I mean to say) whether the person (I'll say person in the absence of a better term) reappears in some murky future in the form of a bird or, let's say, an insect; I'm saying all of this precisely because I feel that the time has come when I must tell you everything I can, that is, everything I know how to tell you as a father and of course because your ignorance stung me two or three days ago when we talked about some of these same things; but it looks like I should have started with that question of yours *Why* FORBIDDEN FOR JEWS, which was bound to make me angry because you're already old enough (oh sweetheart I experienced FÜR JUDEN VERBOTEN up close and personal and learned what it meant when I was fourteen, but that's neither here nor there) to know a few things not just for today and tomorrow but for your whole life and it's best for you to learn them as soon as possible; later on I'm going to come back to what I started telling you about blood (I shouldn't start with blood because it's pretty confusing to me too there's no way simply to say it all just like that) but the issue is that you should learn now that what you have inside you is of Jewish blood and that this is not a thing you'll be allowed to forget or that you can forget; I know, you want to say that you don't see any difference on God's green earth between yourself and Ilonka Kutaj (let's use her as an example) but that's exactly it—*she sees a difference*, and that's more than enough to make you suffer. We, that is your mother and I, have tried hard to make it so that you never felt this difference that would make you unhappy, for you took no notice of it yourself, but other people will always point it out to you (as for us, we didn't need reminding: your mother's parents still lived in the ghetto and my forebears fled Germany after being chased out of their home by pogroms, and I got thrown out of the university in Budapest in 1918 and they spat on me and the small group of other Jewish students too and if the cops hadn't pulled us out of that crowd I wouldn't be talking to you this way today); as I was saying, we tried to keep you from feeling singled out not to mention branded and for that reason we didn't raise you within any sort of religion and I think that aside from the pastries your mother prepares once a year you haven't been exposed to any religious rituals or ceremonies that might distinguish you from Ilonka Kutaj or Ludviga Fuks or the Miletić sisters or from any of your classmates whatsoever; I have to admit that I don't know what your mother might have taught you on her own or how she instructed you and what she talked about with you (given the fact that her mother that is to say your grandmother was Catholic and raised her in her faith; here I must correct myself: I said that your mother's parents lived in the ghetto:

in fact that's a reference to your grandfather on your mother's side) but no one really cares how you pray to God; that's why (I guess) I didn't set much store by that sort of thing and neither your mother nor I, as you've seen, ever concerned ourselves with forms or rituals. That's why I said that you and Ilonka Kutaj pray to the same God but I'd like to communicate to you what I understood that to mean, even though I've already explained something about it to you when we were reading in the Bible, and even I'll say once more that I don't really know what your mother taught you and what kind of views about all these things you might have picked up at school (at your age I had already—I believe I had—asked myself the God question and answered it, I think, according to my own lights—but that's not important at the moment); but look, I want to tell you—and this is the reason I called you here to have this conversation—that my God (I wanted to tell you this immediately and so that's why I digressed into this vague interpretation of religion and blood, for you are after all my sole offspring, you are, I mean, of my blood, just as your own children will be . . .)—my God is simply the incarnation of justice and philanthropy and kindness and of hope";—and she listened to him not knowing whether to reply or to tell him, anyway, that she felt a God inside her who was also something like that but who she wouldn't have been able to define, wouldn't have been able not just then but maybe would never have been able to in her life, had he not said this to her at that time: ". . . a God who bears that name because people gave it to him, but be that as it may, isn't really anything other than a symbiosis of those principles—not to mention of goodness and virtue—that I've just listed for you; only my God is, it seems to me, more beautiful, and better (because in any event every person, every person who believes that he is a good and worthy person, has and should have his own God), and whenever I say out loud or just to myself "God help us" I am actually thinking to myself: "Be just," "Demonstrate love of your fellow men and women," and: "Find hope in your own kindness and in that of your neighbors"; —and she still remembered all this too and etched it into her mind that evening, not knowing at the time whether she was constructing in herself an identical God who was nothing other than the image and incarnation of her father and his words, and it took the fact that her father never returned (the very next day he was taken away during the raid, first to Lampel's cellar and from there to the Danube) for her to realize what he had wanted to say to her and what he was thinking when he spoke of "blood that's eternal, like water, only thicker and harder to see through."—And now she suddenly understood—not without trepidation—those vague pronouncements by means of which her father had wanted to explain to her the meaning of those times in which "the eternity of blood and of the moment" could be sensed. It was this same feeling that was now permeating her to the marrow as the child sucked at her breast, clinging to her, and the moment did indeed have the density of eternity and blood; a great moment when the currents of the past, the future, and the present intersected.

"Žana," she asked all at once, "Do you believe in God?" Then she was quiet because it seemed to her that Žana hadn't heard. Several minutes passed before she responded:

"How about you?" and then after no answer came right away: "Do you believe in God?"

"I don't know," Marija said. "Before I had the baby I didn't think about it."

"But now?"

"Now I'd like to believe in Him. Tonight of all nights I'd like to believe in God"; and then her father was speaking through her: "I mean, in *my* God." Then she paused and there was a dignified silence into which that God was about to come bursting more or less embodied in the form of a newborn child:—"equal parts hope, kindness, mercy, love . . ."

". . . and hate," Žana said.

Marija hardly gave this any thought, as if simply taking the measure of the sword in the hands of that little God-fetish that she had drawn out of her own blood, and said:

"Yes. And hate."

Then Žana said, as if she had seen that absurd naïve deity as it buckled under its massive sword of hope and hatred:

"What would you say if you found that same god in the mouth (and maybe in the mind) of Dr. Nietzsche, for example? Or *Obersturmbannführer* Hirsch?"

"That's impossible!" Marija exclaimed. "This is my God and my God only! No one else's . . ." and then she thought better of it not in the sense of a correction but of a minor addendum to the same thoughts:

"Perhaps my parents' too . . . and my child's."

Then Žana said: "Say it again," and once more Marija dug up quantities of that same clay, and almost in the same amounts, that her father had already turned over in his efforts to construct God in his own image, and to which he bowed: equal parts hope, kindness, mercy, love, and . . . "Hate!" she repeated. And Žana went even further:

"And fear!"

"So be it," Marija said. "Is that your God too? Tell me!"

"No!" Žana said. "No, thank you." Then she added: "That God is too much *in my own image*. Do you get it? In my own image."

"The God of hope and love," Marija said. "So what would you want Him to be like?"

"Like nothing at all!" Žana said. "I want hope and love—without God! Without having to pray or to thank anyone . . . and god cannot be made in my image. Because then it might also resemble Dr. Nietzsche. Or Hirsch. Thanks but no thanks."

"All right," Marija said. "My God's name is Jan. My child."

"*Très raisonnable Dieu!*" Žana said. "Let us pray!"

9

But even before her thoughts could lift her entirely into the future and she could look out over that narrow strip of no-man's-land, for those few hours, even before she noticed the stench of decaying organic matter, she had a presentiment of—almost failing to believe it, for in her thoughts she was already far off into the future—the presence of Polja's corpse. And it drew her back, even if she wasn't fully aware of it, far back to her very origins, so to speak; at any rate, it brought her back from that future into which her thoughts were already marching, with one foot across the thick line of no-man's-land.

What brought her back was hardly the smell, but rather a sensation of decay, a kind of fluid trembling, maybe simply the realization that there was a dead body in the room. And she remembered that old man, long ago, on the Danube.

"Pardon me, pardon me," whispered the old man, leaning or actually lying with his full weight on the elderly woman who was staring blankly ahead in the direction of the green peeling fence. And Marija remembered this: she came back from the Danube and found no one, and it was all clear to her. She took several dresses and a photo album; she even took a bundle of greeting cards and love letters and went dazedly into the street, heading to Aunt Lela's house, and she paid no attention to anyone or anything, not to the police or to the corpses in the snow, but she just walked on with the small cardboard suitcase in her hands that were turning blue; and then she went into Aunt Lela's place and placed her suitcase on the table, opened the spring locks and gave Auntie the album, subsequently catching a glimpse of Mr. Rozenberg *fils*, who—if her mind wasn't playing tricks on her—she had seen in the line-up at the Danube.

When she came in, Aunt Lela said:

"Solomon, don't"; and when he went on as if he hadn't heard her: "For God's sake, Solomon!" but he continued talking with his eyes staring out vacantly and Marija still had the impression that someone else was listening to everything he was saying and not she, although almost all of what she was hearing she had seen herself a few hours earlier at the Danube: she had stood close to the younger Mr. Rozenberg. At least it seemed that way to her. In formations four across, like when they'd stand in line for the showers during a summer heat wave. The trucks kept on arriving. When the line in front of her moved forward a step or two, someone shoved her from behind and she came right up against the green peeling barrier. "It was their turn to take off their clothes." Mr. Rozenberg continued. "The turn of that old man and woman. Naked and wrinkled examples of *Homo sapiens* with sagging breasts and skin that was swollen and blue from age and cold. In this condition, without the clothing or the jewelry by which *Homo sapiens* differentiates itself from the other, less highly evolved species of animals, the whole cohort was after all elemental and antediluvian, with only the occasional gold tooth in a jaw or (less commonly) a few earrings standing as a kind of secret sign of civilization, but these weren't items of enough consequence to be capable of creating any significant distinction between species or individuals, because with work the human hand can become so refined (it suffices to call to mind Thorvaldsen's *Christus*, Leonardo's *Mona Lisa*, and countless violin virtuosos of whom there are, proverbially, many among the Jews) that it, which is to say "the human hand," is in a position to erase this difference wielding nothing more than an ordinary knife, but that isn't what I was talking about, it was those old people (I think they were the Bems, pharmacists, you must've known them) . . ." and Marija remembered the old man whispering, "Pardon me, pardon me," like an over-cranked old street organ and she remembered the way a strong bittersweet smell like a corpse's spread around him, and then the voice of Mr. Rozenberg edged back into her mind, himself talking like an old man in whom every thought was now reconciled to the thought of death but who was himself incapable of grasping whence the *organic* resistance in him was coming, that thing which *biologically* could make no peace with death but rather resisted and grasped and emitted foul odors and juices the way that some animals give off poisonous scents when they're in danger, "as if in him had awakened some embryonic animal that was taking over both mind and man, and his "Pardon me" wasn't really an expression of apology and shame but more fundamentally a desperate expression of dissatisfaction aimed at that animal which had been awakened; for when the mind is reconciled to death and has accepted nothingness, then the utterly exposed and abandoned animal begins by way of an intricate and almost mathematical inversion to fight for its survival and for its right to live (by its own means, of course), and it starts to dominate because the mind has capitulated to death, again according to its own logic that is not the logic of the animal: the animal doesn't know about the complicated laws of probability and death doesn't bear consideration—the animal just wants to live, and that's it"; and right then Marija grasped why it is that around the old man a bittersweet stench of animal and excrement was floating, and then once more she caught the voice of a soldier:

"This one here reeks of cholera."

And she saw the soldier, acting with cynical courtliness, almost like a servant, help the old man out of his greasy trousers, his old-fashioned black vest and his shirt with its stiff, starched collar. All that was visible of the old man were the whites of his eyes, as he whispered "Pardon me, pardon me," as if he were saying "*Lama, lama . . .*" and she heard that *lama* fade more and more as the old man moved away from the group, off to the left a bit, wobbly on his feet and still leaning on the old woman; then Marija steeled herself to hear the volley but when she didn't hear anything she opened her eyes once more and looked left, over to where the voice had died out, and she saw him stoop down, naked, into the snow and understood why he had left the group; the old man was squatting in the snow, with only his head and blue shoulders visible.

"What do you think?" a youngish soldier asked. "Will his mama clean him up when he's emptied himself out? Wipe him off all nice with a lump of snow? That would be fucking hilarious."

"I bet she won't," said a mustachioed one, sticking out his hand. The first soldier shifted his rifle and was about to offer his hand too, but at the last moment he pulled it back:

"Your hands are all Jewed up," he said. "But all right: I'll bet *this* that she *will*," and Marija saw against the backdrop of grubby snow the yellowish metal begin to swing around his hand, hanging from something that she had no way of seeing but knew was a chain, the way that she knew, so to speak, without looking, that the swinging piece of metal was a watch.

And she will always remember this: someone else in her watching all of it (she had slowly sunk into sleepy lethargy and barely even felt the cold anymore): just a few meters in front of her a young woman emerged out of the line-up, almost immediately followed by the dark swirl of a young girl's hair; then she saw the woman bending over the girl and removing her woolen sweater over her curls that bounced and swayed momentarily, and then the white sweater flying in a short arc onto the pile, on top of the old man's black pants and waistcoat and then a light blue dress of poplin, and then the slow descent of stockings and the sliding of petite shoes down from the top of the pile, followed by the woman's trembling as she took the little girl into her arms as if hiding her own nakedness. Lastly the woman lifted up her own reddish-blue foot out of the snow with a slow, hesitating movement, but before she could take a step she turned around as if she were standing on a rotating stage and, still keeping the child pressed tightly against her and sheltering and protecting it with her hands, she said in a voice that sounded dead but did not tremble: "Please, when . . . our turn. My little girl . . . catching cold," after which the soldiers exchanged two or three glances and Marija saw a malicious clean-shaven soldier bow down so far he almost touched the snow and her bluish feet with his forehead and heard him hiss:

"You'll get there in time, I beg you to be patient. In just a bit there'll be kike *tea*, a ton of *tea*. The entire Danube, if you will"; then the polyphonic explosion of the suppressed laughter of soldiers and then the sting of those mouths split wide with laughter on the woman's face from which was peeling layer after layer of reddish-blue and pale green color, and then once more the woman's slow turn and step across the snow as if on a rotating set. And just then, at Aunt Lela's house, listening to the whispering and almost uninflected voice of Mr. Rozenberg *fils*, Marija began to understand everything and to see it all, even those things that had happened ten meters out in front of her, hidden on the other side of the green peeling barrier:

Beyond, at a distance of two or three meters from the cabins, a hole had been smashed in the ice and a plank thrown across it (a plank that was really an old diving board); every now and then a man in civilian clothes (the former lifeguard from the beach) shoved the corpses under the ice with a large gaff, whenever the hole would get clogged; yes, Marija even saw what she was now hearing told for the first time by Mr. Rozenberg: she experienced even that—perhaps because she knew Kenjeri.

"Do you know Kenjeri?" Mr. Rozenberg asked, not looking at Aunt Lela or at Marija or at anyone living but rather at someplace on the ice-sheeted windowpane and on the broken icy surface of the Danube. "Everyone in this district knew him: the community knacker, Kenjeri. I don't actually know his first name. He went by his surname. Well, this old Kenjeri has become head honcho over there. You understand: the man's vocation was a handy one"—and Marija recalled his wolflike jaws and his dirty yellow teeth like a horse's and his sparse moustache and bristly beard and the lit cigarette sticking to his lips while he said to her mother: "What're you gonna do? Business is business" (that happened two or three years ago): Dingo hadn't come home all morning and at noon, just as they were sitting down to lunch, they heard him whining and her mother said: "That's Dingo!" and she stood up so she could see what it was and then appearing in their door was that set of wolf's lips, a cigarette butt on the lower one, saying: "You should watch him better," and what's more: "You have to pay the fine," and right after that were the dirty yellow teeth like a horse's and his saying "business is business"; thus Marija was able to see all of the things that the younger Mr. Rozenberg had seen after he'd already moved beyond the green peeling fence and she could now imagine almost as well as he that face with the bristly beard as Kenjeri pushed a woman's neck into the snow with his heavy boot (and Marija thought that that was the very same woman who had gotten undressed after the old man) and she could see, in the spot where there had once been a face (a face that she could no longer remember), a monstrous stain of concentrated terror, there where before there had been eyes and the lines of a face petrified by cold as when bronze gives off a green patina through its creases; and Marija could remember everything as if she'd experienced it herself: how the boy (judging by his wolfish jaws, the son of that same crook) held the nearly dead woman by the legs and the way the woman writhed like a slaughtered hen when the teeth of the saw tore into the flesh on her side and the way Kenjeri went "prrrr" and then snapped at his son, "Steady, you moron!" and the way his son clenched his teeth and tightened his grip on the woman's legs and then Kenjeri pulling the saw back a bit and pushing it forward and then drawing the serrated tool back forcefully toward himself when the steel found its way down between two vertebrae in her backbone and how, with streams of blood gushing and flooding out into the snow on both sides, the saw began to squish and slip on intestines and flesh. Then, the man snapping at his son once more, "Forget the bitch. I guess her legs won't be running off without her head," and the younger Kenjeri still squeezing the woman's legs and his body twitching and shaking and his father staring at him in amazement, showing his dirty horselike teeth afresh and in protest: "What's wrong with you, you idiot? Is it that you aren't used to blood, or do you actually feel sorry for that whore?" And how he pushed his boy with the handle of the saw and how the boy abruptly dropped the woman's legs and tumbled over into the snow and rolled over onto his belly and submerged his big curly head in the white and bloody snowy mush; then the Kenjeri talking while the boy shook with sobs: "Let's get these here ready and then we'll talk," and then to placate, to instruct, "it's easier to saw than to bust up ice," then the kid slowly, indifferently, getting to his feet without raising his head (just excremental snow in his dark hair), then his wiping his nose with the back of his hand and again picking up the legs of their latest victim, gnashing his teeth with the strain, while his father took hold once more of his tool after having taken the preliminary step of pushing the sundered body through the hole and under the ice; Marija even heard the melody that the wind brought from the left bank of the Danube and she felt each revolution of the gramophone disk leaving behind bloody bites on her body from the steel needle: the "Blue

Danube" waltz was still fashionable at that time; and then all of a sudden Aunt Lela was standing in front of Mr. Rozenberg and making him snap out of it by yelling into his face:

"Enough, Solomon, I beg you," and then, as he stared into space; "Stop, Solomon. Don't go any further with this," and then Marija spoke and was amazed at hearing her own voice in this way:

"I saw it too," and then she wanted to explain to Aunt Lela what it had been like. She remembered: out of the crowd that had been driven into the courtyard of the municipal administration building, a man had singled out a large-breasted girl with freckles right away and ordered her to come with him for an "extra inspection," as he put it, and then a third person turned up, apparently the girl's father, and said that he would go with them.

"I guess you can hold the candle for us," the first man said, kicking the other in the stomach. The girl's father then collapsed to his knees, and so two men in civilian uniforms ran up and knocked him into the snow with their clubs. One of them stood with his foot on the father's neck while the other twisted the prone man's moustache around his fingers and then with a single jerk ripped it off his face and then blood spurted across the snow; the father bellowed and tried to free his neck from the boot but then the first man leaned on his neck with his whole weight; then the second one pulled out a short bayonet that he carried on the belt around his heavy civilian coat barely reaching down to his hips and he sliced off the man's nose. He threw the bloody leftover out in front of the crowd: "Let that be a warning. Don't stick your noses into everything," he said. The one who had grabbed the girl had already dragged her over to the steps from which a heavy machine gun was aimed at the crowd, and they could still see the girl resisting, clutching at the snow, and then, naked and exhausted, she collapsed, seemingly unconscious, and then, while the man removed the belt from around his coat, she let out a scream and dashed back toward the crowd, but the man swung his belt and looped it over her head: "So we're still not ready to calm down, eh?" he said, "Haven't come to terms with your fate yet, have you?": with one hand he tightened the belt around her throat while with the other he twisted her arm and he pinned her bare legs with his boot. She tried to free her throat from the slipknot but the man drew the belt tighter and she dropped into the snow and after that he turned her over onto her back and with great difficulty forced apart her knees as when someone uses his bare fingernails to open up a shell;— and afterward: she remembered how the man got to his feet and tightened his belt again around his short gray coat and how he knelt down next to the girl and whipped out his bayonet, and then the thing Marija didn't see but understood nevertheless: how the man squeezed the girl's cheeks with his left hand until her jaws spread apart and then with two strokes sliced open her mouth on both sides all the way to her ears and then how he pounded on her gold molars with the butt of his gun until he could shake them out into his palm: her head gaped open like some sort of freakish man-eating fish; Marija grasped what she had not seen: for the earrings, no bayonet had been required: when tissue freezes, it becomes brittle and cracks easily.

But she told Aunt Lela none of this. She simply repeated what she had said earlier: "I saw all of it myself, Aunt Lela. I remember everything: from somewhere on the other bank the wind carried across the melody of that waltz: traaaa-la-la-la, tra-la-la-la."

Then she felt a warm wetness coming from the diaper she had wrapped around her child; it penetrated to her skin and delivered her back into the present, which in the following instant would again turn into the past or the future, and she said:

"Is there time for me to do it?" And without waiting for the answer: "For me to get Jan ready."

And even before Žana could say anything at all in response, Marija began unwrapping the wet cloth from the child.

10

Then she had to wrap the baby back up in the diaper that she had dried out on herself. And she tore off a small piece from Polja's sheet and wiped the moisture from her skin. She bundled the child up in a blanket and wrapped it around several times with a narrow strip of linen. Once again she sat down in the straw and leaned her back against the cold barracks wall. The distant thundering of cannon and the rustling of straw from Žana's bed were still all she could hear. And she thought: *I should count.* Thirty was half a minute. Sixty—one minute. Five times sixty . . . How much was five times sixty? Doesn't matter. Maks will be giving the signal in a few moments. The baby is still asleep. She felt the warmth of his soft lips and his hot, slippery tongue on her nipple. In the gloom she could almost make out the elemental mechanism of her own heart pumping the white foamy liquid to the rhythm of her blood into that warm little ring tight around her nipple like a knot. And even before Žana touched her, although she could hear no sound, Marija sensed her proximity. "Now they're going to short out the lights," Žana said. Then Marija let Žana help her get to her feet, although it seemed to her that she was only interested in taking the child. "No," she said, "I can do that myself," but

Marija nonetheless felt faint when she stood up and leaned the weight of her whole body, though without letting go of the child, onto Žana: "I think I can do it myself." They had already reached the door when she heard Žana's barely audible whisper: "Take off your shoes," and then: "give me Jan," and she groped in the darkness for Žana's hands reaching out for her and for the child, and after that she handed Žana the bundle and pulled back her hands as soon as she felt the full weight of the child slide out of her embrace. Her shoulder propped against the wall, she removed one of her shoes and then shifted her weight onto her other leg and took off the other. Without letting go of the heavy boots in her left hand, she stuck out her right through the darkness toward Žana and touched the rough blanket and under it the bound strips of half-wet linen. Then she felt Žana's hand searching for something in the gloom and right after that she felt the weight of the boots vanish as well.

Then Marija noticed a cool draft blowing in from the corridor when the door opened slightly. The hinges on the door creaked a bit like when a board pops from cold in the dead of night. She felt Žana's hand on hers. Žana moved forward. Along the wall. In one hand Žana was holding Marija's boots, while her own, tied together, she carried draped across her other arm at the elbow: the same arm with which she felt Marija's hand draped over the child like a mooring line.

They moved noiselessly, just barely touching the wall with their shoulders. There was no gap to be seen in the thick rubber of the night. This because the electricity had been cut. Otherwise a lightbulb would be burning at the end of the hallway. Marija felt Žana touching the rough surface of the unseen wall with her elbow and stepping forward utterly without sound, like a cat, while she despite her concentration and effort dragged her bare feet over the cold concrete and wet boards, trudging along with uncertain steps, with a cautious gait, like a frightened woman and not like a cat at all. But then a moment came in which when she had succeeded in recognizing herself, and Žana, and the child in Žana's grasp—when she had unwillingly become both a participant and an observer (as when a writer objectifies his or her personal experience even before approaching it as a writer): she suddenly saw herself, from far enough away that one glance took in herself and Žana and the baby but also from nearby enough for her to remain if only for that moment a close but objective observer—seeing how their shadows gleamed white upon the dark nocturnal backdrop: ghosts passing through a cemetery. The mute presence of other rooms, invisible and inaudible, contributed to this feeling like graves yawning open on either side of the corridor, hollowed out of the thick dark wall of the night. Straw rustled somewhere. As if all the women in the rooms were corpses. Polja's corpse. They were all Polja. Then she sensed the almost physical presence of death and of dark green bruises on the flesh of the night. And all at once, from somewhere in front of them, the scent of the wind and the night that was entering through some window left slightly open, a window invisible in the blackness, or through a crack in the glass or a wall, and Marija felt the damp, ice-cold wind waft in on the back of a new quiet, a quiet that had a different taste and smell and specific weight from the dense quiet of the graveyard that she had left behind: at this moment she was taking in the heavy-milky freshness of a child's mouth and the sourish warm smell of urine and moreover the crisp current of the night and the clouds and the unseen stars, scents that penetrated like soft light into her agitated senses made oversensitive by the headlong circulation of her blood. They turned abruptly to the right and she thought it might be possible for Žana to have gotten confused but she didn't say anything because she had more faith at this moment in Žana's resourcefulness than in her own senses. Then Žana's hand stopped squeezing and Marija was left standing motionless, as if rooted to the spot. Without a compass. Blinking. But a faint scratching sound let her know: Žana had picked up a board. "Psss," Žana said in a nearly inaudible hiss. Then she once more squeezed Marija's upper arm and Marija translated this for herself: "Stop." Then Žana pulled her downward and she fell to her knees and bent her head. She understood: the searchlight was already playing its silent scale of uniform notes—do-re-mi-fa-so-la-ti-do—above their heads, and Marija could see now on the wall opposite how through the gap as on white keys its fingers danced and how that resonant light drew nearer and nearer growing into an intense and anxious *fortissimo* that took her breath away. She lay there, clinging to the wall, between Žana and the baby, right at the very edge of the opening that had been made in the floor of the building. Dark square stain just like an open grave. Two or three boards thrown across it. Everything below was swallowed up immediately and dissolved in the gloom that was becoming even thicker. "Give me the child after I let myself down," Žana said and that sentence reverberated in Marija like an echo, *Give me the child after I let myself down! Give me the child after I let myself down!* Then she heard the boards rub against each other as Žana displaced them and then she was trembling and she heard the light thump when Žana touched bottom. Then Marija felt her way to the rim of the opening and leaned over the invisible emptiness. From below—Žana's breathing. She picked up her child, leaned over the breathing, and immediately felt the weight that had weighed down her hands vanishing abruptly as if she had dropped it into the abyss. "Be careful that you don't knock down the boards," Žana said from underneath, from that marvelously confident "underneath" that was giving her the firm footing of damp earth beneath her feet while Marija was still treading the slippery and unsteady boards onstage. Propped up on both elbows and with her body rocking gently, she hesitated for a moment. She could feel that every one of her movements now carried momentous significance for Jan and for Žana as well as for herself. Even for Jakob. Yes, even for him. Dangling over the opening that separated one world and time, one chapter of her history and fate from another, she felt again, without being entirely conscious of it, the denseness of these moments through which passed a nearly tangible current—the past, the present, and the future intersecting, a compact three-way crossroads of time— the dim and dark recorded past cutting across narrow bands of bright new moments and enormous distances sewn with bones and graves (not merely the ones that remained there just behind their turned backs but also all of the graves that she bore in her memory and in her blood, and even all the ones of the unknown people in her family album); the present, swaying slightly in the instant of its birth, issuing forth from the ruptures in the past and, having reached the light of day, heading off to submerge once more in the unknown obscurity of the future: a future that always stands as though on firm footing above the swaying minutes of the present, but which is nonetheless uncertain and unmeasured, dependent upon numerous factors that slice into and blow apart its frames of reference. Then she thought *Polja*, as if someone were reading aloud the inscription on a grave in which the past had been interred, and then she thought, as if some vague ray from the future into which she was letting herself drop had blinded her, *Did Žana get the child out of the way?*—and she flinched the way you'd flinch if you began walking up a stairway you'd only imagined: the ground was just a few centimeters beneath her feet after all. If she stretched out her toes she could touch the ground with her now-dangling legs. But she was afraid that her untied shoes would drop off before she reached the bottom. And then she thought of trying to soften her impact. So she pressed her feet together and held them parallel to the floor along some imaginary horizontal line. The bottom seemed like a deep chasm to her, into which she was supposed to hurl herself with acrobatic skill, or near enough. As though she were jumping straight into the heart of the future. Leaping over the present.

But she only felt a sharp pinch in her heavy shoes. And that was all. But the sensation that followed—and it came immediately after she forced herself to let go and grasped that she was on firm ground—was that every one of these steps she was now taking, after so long a wait, was being taken by her free will alone, free of commands, free of inspections (albeit still accompanied by the fear of sneak attacks), and pervaded by such a sense of ease that she no longer felt her tight boots and the weight of her steps. And she hardly even felt her fear. Or at least not the same fear that she had almost always felt up to the present moment: the fear of events developing so as to carry her along without a single iota of involvement on her part. This new kind of fear, she thought, is the kind that men feel. And Žana, of course. She called it *active fear*. It was something completely different. Her hands were on at least one of the levers controlling these events.

They lay pressed to the damp earth, which had just barely begun to thaw. The baby was lying between them and Marija thought for an instant how he knew nothing about what was taking place around them and within them; he just felt the humid and viscous stain, and this place, where he could barely be seen among his cloth rags, and where his tiny nose was probably a little flushed and reddened by cold, and what's more: the sweet-insipid and thick, sticky taste of warm milk in his oral cavity and sometimes a confused, hesitant rocking. Then she felt hard dirt scattering against her lips and face and its fragile flavor and the nearly imperceptible yet heavy scent of soil that her sense of smell scarcely registered and that anyway you take in more through your tongue and guts: it crackled on her palate and crunched between her teeth while the pores on her skin absorbed it, and then it began to circulate in her blood, which grew thicker because of it and became strong like wine. But she wasn't thinking about all that; it was only a dim, instinctual feeling in her guts as she flattened herself on the ground and tasted the flavor of earth on her lips.

At the same time she felt Žana's hand on her biceps and then came an ultra-quiet whisper: "Be careful the child doesn't start crying," and in addition: Marija felt Žana squirming and breathing and starting to move. Then she wrapped the baby in her arms and dragging herself along on her knees and elbows (the way the females of some species carry their young when they're in danger), head bowed, pushing off on the ground with her left hand, she started following Žana's breathing. From time to time she'd raise her head as if to sniff the air and investigate the obscure space stretching out before her. She sensed above her brow the invisible expanse of the sky and the fresh spaces of the open night. She had no desire to examine what was happening behind her back, where the spotlight must be. She went forward through the darkness creeping behind Žana as if she were climbing along an invisible horizon. As if she were sucking in blood and vital fluids from the very earth and air. Then suddenly she realized that they had reached the wire. Žana slipped through like a cat and she knew: *Žana is on the other side*; then she held the child out and thought *Jan, I have saved Jan*. And then she realized that Žana had laid the baby on the ground and was lifting the wire to allow Marija to pass through. But then, before she could think *The important thing is that Jan is beyond the wire*, she considered, horrified, what it would mean for the child to burst out crying and give them away. And next the child did start to cry and she had just barely gotten herself through the wire and just been able to think once more *This is absolutely the worst moment to die* when they were blinded by the floodlight and she threw herself onto the child and enveloped him tightly and she had only just heard the HALT! HALT! rising up like the voice of death itself as she lay there, half-dead, anticipating with the part of her mind that was still clinging to life the burst of machine-gun fire that would nail her in the back, and at the same time she was seized by a gut feeling: that she should suffocate her baby. That thought jolted her conscience and left her forehead scorched before fizzling out on the tips of her fingers even before she clenched them over the child's mouth. Just as Žana was shaking her she understood the words RUN! RUN! and almost simultaneously a sentence came to her, unclear and at first fully meaningless and hollow, a sentence originating at a distance greater than the one from which Žana spoke: ACH! THEY ARE COMING TO ROB US AGAIN! GET A MOVE ON! NOW! THEY ARE COMING BACK TO LOOT! and then immediately Žana's whisper from nearby making sense of everything in one fell swoop WE ARE SAFE and she sensed Žana's hand squeezing hers and realized that Žana felt her struggling with the thought of suffocating the child and that Žana also realized that it had not yet registered for Marija that they were safe—something that she would only grasp later: the Germans had thought when they heard the baby crying that the escapees must have been people from the surrounding villages (how else to explain their child) who had come to steal supplies (for, since the Allies had been pressing forward, their army in its retreat had laid waste to everything behind it and hunger and cold were advancing too, with women starting to forage and steal everything they came into contact with in order to feed themselves and their children whose fathers were still off making war around the world or who lay piled up in mass graves somewhere in the Urals or on the Volga, at El Alamein or in the Baltic or Pacific Ocean . . .) Then the child, abruptly, ceased crying. Unexpectedly, just as he'd started. Now all Marija could hear was Žana's breathing next to her and she felt the pressure of the other woman's hand. The far-off thudding and rumbling of big guns. And the howling of a dog in the midst of the night.

The child still lay beneath her, but when she came to understand this and lifted her arm and liberated him, he again began to cry with the exultant full-throated voice of a newly freed animal, and from the distance responses came in the form of the rabid barking of a dog and furious artillery volleys. The little creature kept crying in the intense blackness of the night, and his voice rose, twisting like a vine, like the stalk of some miraculously green plant glimpsed among the cavities of skulls, amid the ashes of a fireplace, from out of the entrails of a corpse; and from far away replied the cannon, proclaiming the terrible love between nations.

11

Beside the rutted road at the point where it branched and continued in two directions, Žana discovered a dilapidated sign. This was on the third day of their flight, not counting that first night. They found themselves some five hundred kilometers from Berlin. Most of the distance they had covered in carts, together with masses of refugees. Žana wanted to make it to Strasbourg. Marija was looking for a way to get to Poland where, as agreed upon, she'd wait for Jakob.

"Take the child," Žana said and handed the bundle off to Marija.

It was a crisp foggy morning. Žana hurried down the high embankment and turned the road sign over like it was a corpse. Next to the mud-caked signpost, which had barely been moved from the spot where it had lain, a dark fossilized stripe remained; last year's grass lay in it, withered and pressed as if for preservation. Marija was stamping her feet at the edge of the road, eyeing the pockmarked letters.

"What does it say?" she asked. "What does it say?"

Žana made no reply. She was seated on a stone, with her head bent down low, preoccupied with the bullet-riddled board.

"What does it say?" Marija repeated. "Wipe off the mud. I can't see anything from here. You know, this fog reminds me of . . ."

Žana started to move, lowering herself to her knees. Her head was nearly touching the striped pole. Her arms dangled superfluously, uselessly, at her side.

"What does it say?" Marija asked for the third time. "From here none of it is legible."

Then Žana said, barely loud enough to be heard and without lifting her head:

"It doesn't matter what it says. It's all the same. I can't read it either."

"Then we'll go on in this direction, to the left," Marija said. "I think we have to go this way. To the left. Don't you think so too?"

Once more Žana gave no answer. Her body just quivered.

"Are you crying, Žana? You're crying!" Marija said.

At which point Žana declared firmly:

"Go. Go left. I think that road leads to . . . I don't know where. I don't know what direction this road sign faced originally. But you should go that way. To the left."

"And you?" she said. "What about you?"

So Žana turned her head and raised that small hand of hers that had been hanging there as if unneeded. Marija thought she was going to point to the right. Or somewhere into the fog, across the fields. But her hand, with its finger half-clenched, stopped around the level of her eyes, though she didn't touch them. She went on to say:

"Farewell, Marija! *Adieu* . . . And don't turn around; I implore you: just do not turn around. I believe it'll be easier for you that way."

Marija was still standing at the edge of the road. She watched, panic-stricken, as Žana, now lying on her belly, quaked with sobbing. And suddenly she felt her vision clouding and the baby in her arms becoming heavy as lead . . . And wanting to lean on Žana's shoulder, she embraced only emptiness, and stumbled and then turned and with a frantic burst of pain and strength she began to run along the fog-wrapped road to the left.

Early that evening, fatigued and enervated, she knocked on a door. It was some sort of wayside inn. It looked abandoned to her; no one opened the heavy oak doors for a long time.

"Who's there?" came a man's voice from inside.

She knocked again with her fist.

"What do you want?" asked the same voice, now a little closer.

"Please open up." And she added: "I have a child."

Slowly the door opened, just a crack.

"Refugee?" the woman asked. Marija was astonished when she recognized in the woman's voice the deep baritone that had answered from behind the door.

"I can help you with housework," Marija said. And she added: "Until my husband returns from the front."

"Hmm," the woman said. "Come in. I'm also waiting for my husband. He's in the quartermaster corps."

"Mine is a doctor."

"Right," the woman said suspiciously. "I hear that Germany's gone down the tubes. What do you think?"

"What about you?"

"Well, I think," the woman began, "that the Jews have ruined everything. My husband said that they're to blame for the war. And for everything else."

"Yes," she said: "*every one of them at least brought a nail.*"

"What do you mean, a nail?"

"When they crucified Christ," she said. "That's what it says in the Bible."

"It doesn't say that in the Bible," the woman replied.

"Then it was somewhere else," Marija said.

"Are you a Protestant?"

"Yes," she said. "On my mother's side. My father is a Catholic." She went on: ". . . was a Catholic. He perished on the Eastern Front . . . The Jews killed him."

The woman lit a sputtering oil lamp and placed it on the table. After that she hauled out an old armchair and set it by the stove.

"Put the child down," she said. "I'm going to make a fire. Then we can have our chat."

So she brought in an old door made of oak and with a furious racket began splitting it apart with an axe.

"I don't make a fire very often," she said. "I don't have the wood, and I'm afraid that they'll come bother me if they see the smoke. There are so many of these refugees, and Jews too. Everything has gone to the dogs." Then, abruptly: "Are you hungry?"

"No," she said. "I have just one favor to ask of you."

"I don't have any money," the woman said. "If you stay here to work for me, we'll open a tavern . . . if everything doesn't go to hell."

"No," she said. "That's not what I mean. It's a little paper and a pen. Whatever. So I can get in touch with my husband."

"Don't play the saint," the woman said. She cast a glance at the baby. "That child is not even half a year old," she said.

"Three months."

"See, what did I say? Not half a year old."

"But really," Marija said. "He's an officer."

The woman brought over a greasy old school notebook full of calculations in smeared ballpoint ink. She flipped around in it a bit until she found a blank page.

"Here," she said. "Just don't play the saint."

Marija took the pen and pulled the paper closer to the flame of the oil lamp. Then:

"I'm sorry. I can't do it tonight. I'm tired."

Two or three days later, after the woman had come to trust Marija enough to leave her at home alone (to tell the truth, she did lock the door from the outside) whenever she left for the nearby villages to run some household errands, Marija wrote Jakob this letter:

> The little one is three months old. By day he sleeps in an old armchair next to the stove.
>
> When I have work to do in the yard, Mrs. Schmidt watches him. She still thinks that Jan is a bastard. As soon as you get this letter, let us hear from you so that we know whether you are alive.
>
> I got this address from Mrs. Schmidt. She has promised to get me the addresses of all the displaced person camps.

That was the first letter. After waiting for three months, she wondered if Jakob hadn't received the letter because she had posted it without any stamps. She asked Mrs. Schmidt to lend her the money for stamps.

"All right, all right," Mrs. Schmidt said. "Give me a letter. I'll put stamps on it . . . Just don't you play the saint."

"He'll pay you back, ma'am," Marija said. "He's a doctor. We lost track of each other ten months ago."

That was after three months. In the second letter was this:

> The little one is six months old. He loves to eat dry bread. Mrs. Smith prepares food and I wait on the customers. Sometimes I get chocolate for Jan from soldiers. Mrs. Smith is a little disillusioned. Things haven't gone according to plan for her.
>
> Jakob, I am waiting for you. You taught me how to hope.

In the third letter she transmitted the brief message that their little boy was eight months old and that she thought he looked a lot like him, like Jakob. *He is talking but he isn't walking yet. He's quite the little phenomenon.* This letter was sent to a special section of the Red Cross and to units of the Allied armed forces.

After fourteen days of feverish anticipation, she received a laconic reply:

> Wait for me. I am coming. I love you both.
> *Jakob*

She kissed Mrs. Schmidt on the cheek.

"Fine, fine," she said. "But you're still playing the saint."

"We haven't seen each other for nearly a year and a half. Just imagine: eighteen months!"

"That's nothing," Mrs. Schmidt said. "Mine hasn't been heard from for four whole years. And he wasn't a bad one, believe me. Saturday evenings we would take little excursions. By morning we'd be on top of a hayrick. Then he'd open up his backpack. 'Today, my wife, you will be my guest!' he'd say. Then he would cut two slices of bread and make sandwiches. And pour beer from a thermos into our glasses. Into mine first, then into his . . . Not that I'm not playing the saint here."

12

Jakob lay for the third month in an American hospital several kilometers outside Berlin. Along with general exhaustion and stomach problems, he still had an open fistula on the outside of his left
knee. He had sustained that injury while escaping from the camp
in Oranienburg. That was in November. Two days before the total
evacuation of the camp. He still couldn't eat and he often surrepti-
tiously swapped chocolate for cigarettes. He was smoking a great
deal and taking sleeping pills. During the day he stared at the ceiling and quarreled with the patients who shouted back and forth to
each other and played *préférence*.

"*You're a doctor?*" the director asked him one day, in English. That
was in February. At four in the afternoon, as Dr. Leo was making
the rounds of his patients, Jakob hadn't even noticed the entrance
of the examiners from the medical board. He lay there sprawled
across his iron bed as on a catafalque. He stared at the high white
ceiling. One of his hands hung down next to the bed like a dead
appendage. From time to time he would bring a cigarette up to his
lips, nothing more. Then he'd close his eyes for a moment.

Dr. Leo repeated his question.

"Yes," Jakob said absentmindedly, without taking the cigarette out
of his mouth. His eyes, fogged over with the powerful doses of mor-

phine, were still contemplating the peeling plaster on the ceiling.

"Put out that cigarette," Dr. Leo said in a strict tone. "Our fellow doctor should see to it that he doesn't require further warnings about such things."

Jakob stubbed out his cigarette on the floor, barely moving his hand.

"Where'd you get the cigarettes?"

Jakob gave no reply.

"Where'd you get the cigarettes?" the doctor repeated.

"Screw the cigarettes," he said. "Leave me alone. I've been getting them however I can."

"I explicitly forbade you to smoke," Dr. Leo said.

Jakob fell silent once more. Nervously he closed his eyes. Then he said:

"Why this?"

"What?" the doctor asked.

"All of this," he said. "All this business."

That was in February.

By the next month his condition had only marginally improved. The fistula had ceased festering, but his nerves were even worse. He stopped arguing with the patients. It cost Dr. Leo considerable effort to get so much as a word out of him. He still smoked a lot, but cigarettes were harder to come by now. He wasn't able to put much effort into it. And now he was covering his head and face completely. He couldn't stand sunlight. He demanded that the blinds not be raised during the day, but they didn't listen to him. That's when he started wrapping his blanket around his head. Only at night did he stare at the ceiling. In the dark.

At the end of March, Dr. Leo advised him to start showing some concern for his long-term future. He couldn't stay in the hospital forever. As soon as his wound healed, he'd have to move on.

"I like it here," he said. "I can stop smoking," he said. "If you insist."

"What I'm insisting is that you begin thinking," Dr. Leo said. "That you take care of yourself. Why not write up your experiences, for example? I mean with Nazi medical ethics. Or something along those lines . . . You surely have some valuable, and by that I mean authentic, experiences to share."

Jakob waved him off with a barely perceptible movement of his hand.

"Shall I bring you some writing supplies?"

"No," Jakob said. "Why?"

"You have to find a project. Whatever it is. Play chess at least. Or cards. Anything at all," Dr. Leo said.

No answer came. He didn't even gesture with his hand.

Then Dr. Leo said:

"Do you have anyone? *Parents or wife?*"

"No one," he said. "So much the better."

"Shall I have them issue you a passport?" Dr. Leo asked. "What are your thoughts about that? So you can head for Palestine? Or America?"

"No," he said. "Not Palestine . . . I've had enough of all that."

"For the US, then," Dr. Leo said calmly. "There's none of that there."

"None of what?"

"What you fear: scars. No one will hassle you to write your memoirs," Dr. Leo replied with a smile. "America is where scars get

128

lost in the crowd. Do you understand? At least there are women there who are still in one piece. And children, of course."

"All right," Jakob said. He turned toward the doctor: "I agree," he went on listlessly. "Scrounge up a passport for me, if it means so much to you."

Dr. Leo promised that it would be ready as early as the middle of April. At the latest by May. Jakob hardly grew any more upbeat. He would take up residence in some quiet spot in Canada. Anywhere. The only thing he cared about was crossing the ocean. That, perhaps, would be his purgatory.

On the day, the last day of March, when he received a letter from Marija and Jan, he was lying in his bed next to the open window. His head was propped up slightly on his pillow. He was watching the flickering of the sun across the white varnish on the opposite wall. He was imagining a large ship gliding across the Atlantic in calm, sunny weather. It was about four o'clock in the afternoon, just before the doctors checked in on their patients. Before they came, the mail was handed out. It was going on right now. All the patients, including those on crutches and the ones in wheelchairs, were in the sun-filled lobby of the building where the mail was usually distributed. Only one other person stayed behind in the ward with Jakob: a boy who had recently had an amputation and been delivered to the ward the night before.

"There's some mail for you," Danijel said, laughing and then straining as he pushed against the narrow planks on the door to make his wheelchair move. One of his legs had been removed—a victim of the Institute of Scientific Research. His voice was unnaturally scratchy and his hair had fallen out. Jakob recognized the symptoms of forced sterilization by means of the "special method."

"They've already called your name three times," the boy said, rowing with broad strokes across the smooth parquet floor. "I assumed you were asleep . . . Otherwise you would have definitely heard them."

Jakob started, and then reached out apathetically for the letter. He quickly scanned the envelope.

"Danijel," Jakob said as he grabbed the boy by the upper arm. Danijel still had a trace of a smile on his face, and he was staring at Jakob. "Have you ever watched someone be resurrected?"

Now Danijel's little smile was mournful.

"No? Watch me, then . . . First a person starts to cry, as you can see. Then he drops his letter. It's like when someone has gone hungry for a very long time. You can't gorge yourself right away. Then one lights a cigarette," Jakob said, and he offered the pack to Danijel. "There you have it. This, this is what it's like. You see . . . It'll be you one of these days."

Dr. Leo too expressed his surprise.

"How are you feeling, compatriot? *You're an American now . . . Aren't you?*"

"Excellent, Doctor," Jakob said. "I'm imagining my trip across the ocean . . . But, of course, I'm not alone . . . Do you know what I mean?"

"Bravo," Dr. Leo said. "But you've forgotten again that you aren't allowed to smoke."

"Indeed," Jakob said. "Forgive me, but I thought that, on the deck of a transatlantic liner, smoking was permitted." Dr. Leo smiled contentedly.

That same day, in the early evening, Jakob left his room unobserved. Most of the patients were asleep. Out on the terrace he ran into no one but Danijel.

"Farewell, Danijel," Jakob said in a low voice. They shook hands.

"Where to, Doctor?" the kid asked.

"Do me a favor, Danijel," Jakob said. "Give Dr. Leo my apologies and tell him I said thanks for everything."

The boy looked as if he understood, so Jakob added only: "But not until tomorrow. No earlier . . . Understand? . . . Not before then."

"Have a good trip, Doctor," the boy said and began to row his wheelchair across the smooth parquet floor.

13

EPILOGUE

It was on a humid day in summer that Jakob and Marija paid another visit to the camp. Jan had turned six years old, and he was wearing short pants of white linen and a light-colored shirt. He was a thin boy, with a look of curiosity and mild anxiety on his face. He had Jakob's demeanor and the shapely, intelligent eyes of his mother. Usually an especially lively and inquisitive boy, he was now tight-lipped and furtive—perhaps just fatigued from the journey. But, ever since the bus stopped at the edge of the camp (it was a special tourist bus from a Warsaw company and it had been rented by the association of former prisoners for the commemorations of the anniversary of the liberation) and since the ceremonies and speeches had begun, accompanied by stifled tears and audible sobs, he had suddenly fallen silent. This left Marija worried. Without waiting for the ceremony to conclude or for the choir to intone its set of mournful songs, among them "The Girl I Adore," Marija took the child by his hand and led him away from the crowd. She did this as a bus carrying American tourists drew up and, with its loud honking, drowned out the solemn invocation of "The Girl I Adore." The eyes of the former camp inmates dimmed with reproach at this failure to respect the suffering and memories of others. Nevertheless their agitation grew even greater when the bus's horn stopped blaring and was replaced by a hoarse bass voice from its radio. A man was singing in raspy tones about how great it was to be alive: "*C'est si bon . . .*" This brief, unpleasant confusion was sufficient for Marija, Jan, and Jakob to slip away unobserved. Marija noticed just then that Jan was crying quietly. "Didn't my little man promise me he'd be a hero and not do any crying?" she asked. She already felt a touch of regret at having brought the boy along. Although the two of them had decided to show Jan everything that wasn't too upsetting, she was sorry now that she had talked to him about the camp, even though what she had said was mild and sanitized, like some kind of fairy tale. But she had wanted to impress on Jan's very brow the stamp of martyrdom and love: the same symbol that she and Jakob had made of their suffering. But Jan was meant to profit from all that. And Marija was proud of this mission of hers: to transfer to Jan the joyousness of those who were able to create life out of death and love. To bequeath to him the bitter happiness that had resulted from suffering that he had never felt and would never personally experience, but suffering that needed to be present in him as a warning, as joy: like a memorial obelisk.

In the display cases of the camp museum there are purses and wallets made of human skin. *Made in Germany.* Human skin from the tannery; when it's thoroughly dried out, it resembles parchment. And any blank white sheet of paper inflames the human imagination, for all people are artists and are eager to leave some trace of themselves on earth. It was probably that very fact which impelled the *Übermensch* to inscribe his initials on this completely anonymous human skin, in this ideally white spot, thereby convincing us irrefutably of his artistic inclinations. *Ars et artibus,* art and delight, as venerable old Horace proclaimed, have always been among the essential characteristics of each and every worthy creation. And love is, as always, only a stimulant. Therefore one should not wonder that an *Übermensch*, in the form of some artistically inclined SS officer, would choose nothing other than a lady's toiletry case as the object of his craft. To give such a case of human skin to a lady of Aryan blood would mean not only that he was confirming, clearly and palpably, his personal power and artistic proclivities, but also demonstrating and proving to the lady in question that human life is an extremely ephemeral phenomenon; human skin is neither as expensive nor as valuable as one might think. And, furthermore, if the stamp of the artist (that is to say, of a man who is no stranger to metaphysics) is imprinted on the bag in the form of a drawing or watercolor depicting a kitschy and infantile boat, sails filled with wind (a symbol of higher, metaphysical powers) or a stenciled lily (a symbol of bodily and spiritual innocence), then the effect is full and complete. The *Übermensch* triumphs in love and in art.

Two American women, faces freckled and wrinkled, sporting sunburns, big straw hats like chandeliers, and loud, multicolored nylon dresses, labored, with the help of a dictionary, to decipher untranslated details about the mattresses stuffed with women's hair. Locks of hair of various colors, from blonde to red to black, mingled together in a heap and exuding sadness like the golden crowns of famous queens, princesses, or virgins found on a battlefield or in a museum basement. But the essential characteristic of an *Übermensch* is that he is not sentimental; he knows how to counter the metaphysics of death with the hard, forceful physicality of life. He knows how to take from death almost as much as he gives it. *Übermensch*—the very word mocks death. Such a man takes bone to make fertilizer, turns skin into purses and wallets and lampshades, produces mattresses and pillows from . . . hair. It is only the vapor of human vanity and nullity that is sacrificed to death. I will teach you life—thus spoke Zarathustra.

Then a group of noisy kids arrived. They were wearing leather shorts and suspenders. One of them carried a bouquet of foxtail—a symbol of respect. They paused in front of the pile of eyeglasses. In this pile the size of a haystack there were glasses of all sizes and shapes. There were iron frames already beginning to show rust. The frames with cracked or shattered lenses bore more of a resemblance to the holes in a bare skull than to a bit of old metal. One of the boys raised a camera up to his eyes. It clacked against the glass in his own spectacles. The boy, however, remained blind to analogies and coincidences. Jan had already noticed that. Pointing to the heap, he asked, "Are these glasses the same as the ones that the young man in short pants is wearing?"

Marija stared at the yellowish, downy hairs on the boy's legs.

"They are," she noted. "They're the same." She knew what would come next, and she was already feeling uncomfortable. Jan said: "Well . . . Why—?" But she didn't allow him finish his question because she dreaded the answer.

"These are broken," she said, "and that's why they got thrown out." The young man's camera clicked and then he carefully wiped it off with a deerskin cloth and put it away. Next he crouched down in front of the pile. Only his head could be seen; he took off his glasses. From the pile he extracted another pair, with steel frames and one discolored and cracked lens. He put them on his nose. "*Hu-hu! Ich bin Jude! Ich bin Jude!*" Then the sharp clatter of the glasses as they were tossed back. And the sharp, needle-like sound of glass splintering, mixed with a peal of unruly laughter.

"*Hu-hu! Ich bin Jude!*"

Jakob had stopped in front of the cabinet in which the achievements of Nietzsche's Center for Scientific Research were on display. In alcohol-filled jars floated freakish little unborn children, monsters of artificial crossbreeding and experimentation. This was too much for Jan. So Marija led the boy on further, letting Jakob know by way of silent gestures. A group being led by a docent stopped in front of the cases with the little malformed creatures and listened to the monotone explanation, as professional and as indifferent as could be. When Marija heard the cicerone's voice starting up again behind her back, she tugged on Jan's hand. "Same disgusting old song," she said to herself. "You drop in five marks and the money goes right to his tongue. And the record starts spinning. Lazy, indifferent. Hideous, stupid Tower of Babel . . . All for five marks." Then she saw that the disgusting old organ grinder was right in her path. So when the visitors, including Jakob, started shuffling their feet and snapping photos, she let go of Jan's hand and walked without a word into another room. She wanted to be alone, right then and there. (There are moments when selfishness and loneliness can prevail over love.) She couldn't bear to hear the guide's voice or the footsteps of people entering a place of execution as though it was a bazaar. It was cool and mostly dark in the room she had entered. The touch of the cool air was pleasant to her sweat-covered palms. She was out of range of the guide's voice now. That allowed her to calm down. She could sense that Jakob and Jan were moving toward her solitude, toward the open door. They were holding hands. Without turning her head she could see the two of them, Jakob and the child. Jan was looking at the welter of unfathomable, fantastical objects without daring to ask anything at all. And Jakob still held him by the hand, tense in anticipation of questions and preoccupied with preparing answers. They had agreed to show the boy everything he could comprehend and take in without getting terrified. But at this point Jakob would have preferred for the child to ask no questions of him. Marija would be better at explaining it all to him.

Then the guide's steps were audible once more (he had a peculiar, irregular gait), and his dreary voice too. It ripped into Marija's consciousness along with the realization that Jakob was going to leave it to her to satisfy Jan's curiosity. She thought: he needs to get the child out of here. The three of them should have been alone in this place. Without an audience. And without that guide. They shouldn't have come during the tourist season. Later would have been better. At the start of winter. Or in late fall. They lived in Warsaw. It wasn't far. Jakob worked in a hospital. She gave German lessons.

Then she heard Jakob's voice.

"Marija," he said. "I have a surprise for you."

He hadn't shut the door. Only his head poked inside. It was still just as dark in the room. Music from a radio reached them. It seemed to her that the tune was similar to "The Girl I Adore." But it was in fact just a march. Or a waltz, maybe.

"Are you crying?" Jakob asked. "You are!"

She pulled out a handkerchief to wipe her eyes:

"It's nothing," she said. "It's . . . I just felt depressed all of a sudden. What did you want to tell me? Jan must be . . ."

Jakob was embarrassed.

"Right," he said. "He's talking with the guide."

He pushed the door open all the way and Marija caught sight of Jan and the docent. They were standing together as if in front of a curtain on a stage. The two of them. Jan and the guide. Holding one another by the hand.

When the door swung open, they bowed to her. As if they'd been practicing. Wreathed in grins. "May I introduce you, at last, to your *deus ex machina*?" Jakob said. "This is Maks."

Then the two of them, the child and the cicerone, started toward her. The man was lame in his right leg. Jakob stood to one side. With a mournful smile on his face.

Beograd–Herceg Novi, 1960

TRANSLATOR'S AFTERWORD

Although the great Danilo Kiš (1935–1989) also wrote poetry and drama, he is certainly best known in Central Europe, the Balkans, and the world of translation for his novels, such as *The Attic* (1962), *Garden, Ashes* (1965), and *Hourglass* (1972), as well as his sets of interlocking stories—themselves considered rather novelistic by some readers—such as *A Tomb for Boris Davidovich* (1976) and *The Encyclopedia of the Dead* (1983). With the publication of this novel, *Psalm 44*, and the simultaneously published stories of *The Lute and the Scars*, most of Kiš's fiction has now seen the light of day in English. Significant quantities of his other work have not yet been translated, and hence they have unfortunately not yet factored into the ways most of us categorize, or interact emotionally with, Kiš and his work. Our interest in Kiš's already intriguing persona, views, and books (the elegiac, almost lapidary prose; the pointed documentary and narrative experiments; and his evocation of history as marginalization, peril, and loss) seems likely only to deepen and become more nuanced as more of his works become available. Ultimately, to access and take account of Kiš's humor, paradoxes, disdain for party politics, sense of the "revolutionary" in art, and even his linguistic patriotism or at least his acknowledged South Slavic heritage, is to treat Kiš in a responsible and more comprehensive way. It also gives us more to appreciate than just Kiš the restless and sharp-witted postmodernist, polemicizing about his work in the 1970s, or Kiš the "good Serb," or the "un-Serb," whose writings were revived in the West in the 1990s as people strove to understand the madness erupting in the wars of Yugoslav succession.

Psalm 44 is, above all, a story about a young family during the Holocaust. Marija, Jakob, and little Jan are at Auschwitz or its associated camps, and most of Kiš's narrative about the death camp is devoted to a depiction of the miserable and brutal life in its women's section. Some of the chapters are presented as stream-of-consciousness narrative; others contain lengthy flashbacks; some passages combine the two techniques, often with abrupt returns to the central narrative set in the camp. A reader gets the impression that the characters, like the author, are trying to make sense of the unprecedented events (prejudice and discrimination and persecution in the eyes of a child in the Vojvodina, at first, moving to the mind-numbing terror of the Final Solution) and to find a mode of expressing the experiences of the Shoah in words. We also find brief historical and philosophical references to the relationship between Judaism and Christianity, and comments on the hollow enterprise that was "Nazi science," on the nature of Holocaust commemoration in the postwar period, and on West German and American reactions to such remembrance.

The plot and chapter structure are relatively simple, even if the texture of the emotional and allusive prose is not. The characterizations are unique because of the unexpected and fitful ways the relationships and personalities are revealed to us. The characters fight, often in small but significant ways, to maintain a sense of human dignity.

Kiš had good reasons for writing about the Holocaust, and an unenviably close vantage point for doing so. He was born in the northern Yugoslav city of Subotica (Hungarian: Szabadka) on February 22, 1935. His home region, technically the Bačka but commonly referred to by the more expansive designation of the Vojvodina, had been part of medieval Hungary before being captured by the Ottomans in early modern times; it then became part of the Habsburg Empire for well over two hundred years before World War I; after the collapse of Austria-Hungary in the Great War, this multi-ethnic, multi-confessional region, which is home to Serbs and other South Slav groups as well as Hungarians, Slovaks, Ruthenians, Germans, Roma, Jews, and others, was included in the new country of Yugoslavia. Kiš's mother, Milica Dragićević, was an Orthodox Christian from Montenegro, and he spent the immediate postwar years in that Yugoslav republic, following his repatriation from Hungary. Kiš's father, Eduard, was a Hungarian Jew. A railroad inspector with a difficult and in some ways troubled personality, Kiš's father also had something of the visionary and philosopher in him; both his obscured personality and his tragic fate dominate the affective world of many of Kiš's works. The family tried, with mixed results, to escape the rising tide of anti-Semitism on both sides of the shifting Hungarian-Yugoslav border in the late 1930s and early 1940s. When the war finally ended in 1945, Kiš, his mother, and his sister Danica were leading a deliberately low-key but physically and emotionally very difficult life in rural southern Hungary; his father had been rounded up for forced labor and later was deported and then killed by the Nazis. The war years, the Holocaust years, the years of exposure and hatred and invidious otherness, are famously portrayed in Kiš's magisterial novel *Hourglass*, but they are also an indispensable constituent element of his poetry, the untranslated short stories, and in his drama *Night and Fog*.[1]

This novel, then, is obviously one that was very important to Kiš peronally. But it was an early novel, written in 1960 and first published in 1962, paired with *The Attic*, which he had started in 1959 but also completed in 1960. As a work of relative youth, written when the author was in his mid-twenties, the book exhibits certain lapses or excesses, infelicities or imbalances, the correction of which gives us, in his later works, insight into Kiš's artistic and intellectual evolution. In his interviews, Kiš himself would occasionally wax wry or wistful about the novel, revealing a guarded or even critical attitude toward *Psalm 44*. Kiš based the novel on a true story reported in the newspapers at the time, and he wrote it as part of a competition held by a Jewish cultural organization in Belgrade. He felt, though, that the novel made its points too directly, without enough lyricism[2] or "ironic detachment."[3] But he believed that the book addressed a need in postwar Yugoslav literature, with its "latent resistance to Jewish subject matter"[4] and, one supposes, its Manichean depictions of the war aimed at mo-

---

1. "Night and Fog," trans. John K. Cox, *Absinthe: New European Writing* 12 (2009): 94–133.
2. "Seeking a Place under the Sun for Doubt," in *Homo Poeticus: Essays and Interviews*, ed. Susan Sontag (New York: Farrar, Straus, Giroux, 1995), 186.
3. "Life, Literature," in Sontag, *Homo Poeticus*, 249.
4. "Seeking a Place under the Sun for Doubt," in Sontag, *Homo Poeticus*, 186.

bilizing and militarizing Yugoslav society. Kiš also saw the book, and his other Holocaust writings, as the first bookend of what I call his great project of convergence—his unmasking of the twin "totalitarian" leviathans (or ideological dictatorships) of the twentieth century, Nazism and Soviet communism.

Perhaps Kiš was thinking of the prominent role of his *deus ex machina*, or of the heavy-handed recasting of Mengele as "Dr. Nietzsche," when he later referred to the book's plot as "too charged, too overwrought."[5] But ultimately the graphic brutality of some of the scenes in *Psalm 44*, as well as the unexpected and highly evocative details—the interplay of light and wire and walls, or some of the bodily sensations of the protagonist, Marija—help key the reader's emotions to the pain and gravity of the subject. And Kiš's portrayal of life in the Vojvodina during the heyday of fascism is a rare (and beautifully written) testimony about this under-studied regional chapter of the one huge Holocaust. Native fascism, local collaboration with the Nazis, myths of ancient ethnic hatreds, the envy and insecurity that lie at the psychological root of anti-Semitism, the violence against women—the presence of these historical themes in the narrative makes *Psalm 44* far more important than any hasty characterization of it as "provincial" might vouchsafe. No part of the Holocaust was a sideshow, just as the Shoah itself was not a footnote but rather a necessary condition of and an integral component of the Nazis' geo-strategic and military aims.

The first things one notices about *Psalm 44* are the title and the book's stream-of-consciousness style. The forty-fourth psalm

---

5. "Life, Literature," in Sontag, *Homo Poeticus*, 249.

is one in which an ancient voice laments bitterly the fate of his or her people and offers no little challenge to God for this tremendous time of trial:

> Thou hast made us like sheep for slaughter,
> and hast scattered us among the nations.
> Thou has sold thy people for a trifle,
> demanding no high price for them . . .
> Thou hast made us a byword among the nations,
> a laughingstock among the peoples.
> All day long my disgrace is before me,
> and shame has covered my face.

The interior monologues challenge us to make sense of the same situation that Marija is trying to understand. One might even say that Kiš, as author, is grappling with credibility, credulity, and expression just as we, and his characters, are doing: what is occurring is so brutal, so frightening, so wrong, and so new that simple language would be insufficient for it. The reckless punctuation and changes in tense—reproduced at least in part in this translation—and the flashbacks and occasional double flashbacks, along with the compound nouns, some of which even incorporate proper nouns, such as "doll-sleeper" and "fate-Jakob," all represent attempts to create an emotional and intellectual space in which we might have a fighting chance of understanding something of what the characters are facing.

There are many unforgettable, carefully crafted scenes in this novel. We have Anijela in her coffin; the almost unspeakable savagery against civilians on the banks of the icy Danube; the approach of Allied artillery "demolishing the concrete parapet of passive waiting and resignation to fate"; the description, full of lyricism and surprise, of Marija's personal encounter with her own *deus ex machina* in Chapter 5, and her bold assertion of solidarity by means of the transferred memories and feelings of "heroes or virgins" in the following chapter; the harmonization of the combined power of cinematic experience and religious imagery in a flashback to a small village in the prewar Vojvodina; and Marija's mesmerizing discussion with her parents about the meaning of a public transportation ban for Jews in their provincial capital, Novi Sad. Then, finally, toward the end of the book, we hear and even see (for Kiš combines the imagery) the cry of the child Jan, at once unifying and splitting the world, its proverbial hopefulness downplayed and only faintly present behind the jagged profusion of what Kiš designates, specifically yet with perfect poetic touch, as a world of rabidity, entrails, ashes, fury, and skulls, skulls evoking the terror of some kind of medieval *memento mori* or the immeasurable forgotten carnage of mass death. All these images draw us deeper and deeper into the scene, sucking out the oxygen from our heads, plunging us into an emotional vacuum, and they are then followed by a statement so simple and clear in formulation that its erudition and irony create emotion right where we thought no more was possible. Kiš once again evokes war, the advance of foreign forces, artillery—disembodied but Soviet, lethal but promising rescue—"proclaiming the terrible love between nations."

There are many admirable and emotionally powerful works of Holocaust literature. All kinds of people have written such works:

from victims and observers of the events of the 1930s and '40s, to relatives and loved ones of victims after the fact, to artists with no direct connection to those events who want to engage with the Holocaust's maelstrom of deep and painful emotions and its microcosm of plots and themes. What, however, makes certain works of Holocaust literature "great"? This historian and translator admits to a preference for literary works in which the challenges of form somehow evoke or parallel the challenge of the content; I am also drawn—in what is probably a peril of the historian's trade—to works that reflect some of the historiographical richness of the remarkable field of Holocaust studies: for example, such topics such as collaboration; resistance; struggles of memory and representation; non-German anti-Semitism; and murder outside the camps, outside the ghettos, and outside Poland and Germany. In other words, since the popular understanding and media tropes of the Holocaust leave so much of these chapters of history, and the scholarship based on them, unplumbed, books that engage our minds and our ethical faculties in *less common ways* would seem to be worthy of particular attention. *Psalm 44* is this kind of book.

JOHN K. COX, 2012

TRANSLATOR'S NOTES

p. 58   *Ja, ja, ich verstehe*: "Yes, yes, I understand . . . But I don't
         think she's it. Too small. Her pelvis is like a child's. But in-
         sofar as my esteemed colleague considers her sufficiently
         attractive . . ."

p. 58   *Du, Abschaum!*: "You, scum!"

p. 58   *mutan gemišt, mongrel*: Kiš uses a highly unusual pejora-
         tive, which might be translated as "muddy mixture."

p. 97   *Let us pray*: Russian in the original: "*Pomolimsja!*"

p. 101   *Lama, lama*: "Why, why" in Hebrew and Aramaic.
         Probably a reference to the phrase uttered by Jesus on the
         cross, as recorded in Matthew 27:46 and Mark 15:34: "My
         God, my God, why have you forsaken me?"

p. 119   *some five hundred kilometers from Berlin*: the Serbian text
         actually locates Marija and Žana a rather unlikely five
         hundred kilometers "*northwest* of Berlin."

p. 125   *on top of a hayrick*: Kiš has "on top / at the summit of [the] Hainkorn," leaving his translator and editors to puzzle over whether this is meant to be a (misspelled or fictional) German mountain or else a pile of wheat hay (German *Einkorn* = "single-grain," wild wheat).

DANILO KIŠ was one of Serbia's most influential writers and the author of several novels and short-story collections, including *A Tomb for Boris Davidovich*, *Hourglass*, and *Garden, Ashes*. He died in 1989 at the age of 54.

JOHN K. COX is professor of history and department head at North Dakota State University. His translations include books *The Attic* and *The Lute and the Scars* by Danilo Kiš, as well as short fiction by Kiš, Ismail Kadare, Ivan Ivanji, Ivo Andrić, and Meša Selimović.